Victoria stood by the fire, feeling empty, defeated, lost.

After a while, she sat down, hugging her knees to her chest, wishing she'd never left home, that she'd never gotten into this mess.

She was, as Jarred reminded her, in his world. He was lord and master here, and she was completely dependent on him.

Whether Jarred would actually act like a wild savage beast or not, she had to acknowledge that he had the potential to do so. How could she hope to keep him at bay forever?

And he wasn't the only problem. She hadn't resisted when he kissed her, and she'd gotten aroused before she finally stopped him. They would be intimate, whether out of mutual weakness or his unwillingness to stay away from her.

She had no choice. She would have to get far enough from the cave that she could flag down the helicopter. And if the chopper didn't return, she would just have to walk out of the mountains.

Dear Reader,

What is more appealing, more enduring than *Cinderella, Beauty and the Beast* and *Pygmalion*? Fairy tales and legends are basic human stories, retold in every age, in their own way. Romance stories, at their heart, are the happily ever after of every story we listened to as children.

That was the inspiration for our 1993 yearlong Lovers & Legends miniseries. Each month, one book is a fairy tale retold in sizzling Temptation-style!

February brings Janice Kaiser's *Wilde at Heart,* a moving and adventurous adaptation of the beauty and beast fairy tale. Initially, heroine Victoria Ross regards the tale of Jarred Wilde simply as great material for a book. When she finally locates Jarred, he touches more than just her imagination!

In the coming months, we have stories from bestselling authors Leandra Logan—*The Missing Heir* (*Rumpelstiltskin*), Glenda Sanders—*Dr. Hunk* (*The Frog Prince*), Kelly Street—*The Virgin and the Unicorn* (unicorn myths) and Gina Wilkins—*When It's Right* (*The Princess and the Pea*).

We hope you enjoy the magic of Lovers & Legends, plus all the other terrific Temptation novels coming in 1993!

Birgit Davis-Todd
Senior Editor

P.S. We love to hear from our readers.

Wilde at Heart

Janice Kaiser

Harlequin Books

TORONTO • NEW YORK • LONDON
AMSTERDAM • PARIS • SYDNEY • HAMBURG
STOCKHOLM • ATHENS • TOKYO • MILAN
MADRID • WARSAW • BUDAPEST • AUCKLAND

Published February 1993

ISBN 0-373-25529-2

WILDE AT HEART

1

VICTORIA ROSS FELT a sense of anticipation as she drove into the little mountain town. For months she had been studying Dr. Walther's research on the wild man of Edgar, Washington, and the details had gripped her imagination as vividly as the fairy tales her grandmother had read to her as a child. His story was an anthropologist's dream come true. While the professor had taken the wild man almost for granted, concentrating more on the folklore of the region, she had become passionately interested in the mysterious creature himself.

She pulled over and parked on the deserted main drag. As Victoria got out of the car, she listened to the wind howling down from the mountains, making the pines moan and the wood smoke bend from chimneys. The air felt as if it were coming right off the snow-capped peaks, although it was still November, and winter was officially several weeks away.

She zipped her parka to her chin, tugged a stocking cap over her light brown hair and stared at the mountains, shivering at the thought that *he* was up there somewhere, alone. Sighing, she took her briefcase from the back seat, slammed the car door shut and glanced around. There were only three vehicles on the street besides her own—two pickups parked in front of what appeared to be a run-down bar across the way, and a battered old car farther up the street.

The town's economy was reeling from hard times. The shops looked vacant, the streets deserted. She remembered the professor telling her that the surrounding forests had been logged out and those who had remained in the area had to scratch out livings from the sporadic tourist traffic on the highway, or make do on social security checks.

Dr. Walther's descriptions had made the town seem very real to her. So real that as she walked along everything felt very familiar. After passing several empty shops, Victoria came to a building with light shining through the plate glass window. Stenciled on the glass were the words, "City Hall." Through the venetian blinds she could see an elderly woman sitting at a worn wooden desk. She was smoking a cigarette and reading a newspaper.

Victoria went inside. The woman was obviously surprised to see a strange face and immediately put down her paper. "Afternoon."

"Hello," Victoria said. "I'm looking for a Willard Johnson. I believe he's the mayor."

The gray-haired woman, who wore a bulky beige cardigan that appeared two sizes too large for her, smiled. "I'm afraid you're about three months too late, dear. Willard's been gone since September."

"He left town?"

"Only as far as the cemetery. His drinking finally got to him. I'm the city clerk and sort of in charge," she said. "Name's Anna Norton. Something I can do for you?"

"I don't know. Mr. Johnson's name was the only one I had."

The woman took a last drag on her cigarette before stubbing it out. She glanced at the briefcase in Victoria's hand. "Some kind of official business?"

"Not really... My name is Victoria Ross. My advisor at the University of California, Dr. Walther, did some research in Edgar last summer. I'm here to follow up on it."

"Oh, yes, the professor. I remember him. He ran all over town, sticking his tape recorder in everybody's face." She gave Victoria a warning look. "I hope that isn't what you've got in mind to do, young lady."

"Not at all. I'm here because Dr. Walther has had a stroke and is unable to continue his work. He showed me the research he'd done on the wild man of Edgar and I became fascinated with it. So, I just had to visit."

"Visit is one thing. Opening old wounds is another."

Victoria paused, choosing her words carefully. "Dr. Walther indicated that some people aren't disposed to talk about the wild man."

"The wild man, as you call him, was an ordinary boy, a good kid who had some bad things happen to him. It was a sad time in this town's history—not one most people want to relive."

"But Mr. Johnson—"

"Willard Johnson had a fancy notion he could turn Jarred Wilde into a kind of Bigfoot, and bring tourist money to town by playing up the legend. He saw your professor as a way to promote his scheme. It was just a publicity stunt."

"But Jarred Wilde *is* real, Mrs. Norton. He's not a mythical creature like Bigfoot."

"Was real, you mean. He's been dead for fifteen years now, and it's a damned shame everyone don't let him rest in peace. Not that I'm not blaming you personally, understand. It's really the fault of the folks who insist on spreading tales. That's what brings people like you and the professor around. For years it was newspaper men. Now it'll be scholars."

A potbelly stove against one wall kept the room very warm. Victoria yanked off her stocking cap and ran her fingers up under the hair at the back of her neck, then unzipped her parka.

"Take off your coat, if you want to sit for a spell," the woman said, gesturing toward the straight wooden chair next to the desk. "I don't mean to sound like a bitter old lady, but I just don't like the way of Jarred's being used."

Victoria set down her briefcase on the corner of the desk then removed her gloves and her coat, which she hung on the back of the chair. The woman watched her with straightforward curiosity that she had always associated with small-town life in places like Siskiyou County, where she'd grown up. In fact, Anna Norton reminded her of her own grandmother.

"I have no intention of stirring up trouble, Mrs. Norton," Victoria said, sitting on the edge of the chair.

"What is it you want then?" the woman said, fiddling with the pack of cigarettes lying on the desk.

"Dr. Walther was doing a study on the way tales reflect a society's values and beliefs. My interests are different." She paused for a moment, then leaned forward. "I've come to Edgar because I want to learn all I can about Jarred himself."

The old woman took a cigarette from the pack, fumbling it with arthritic fingers. "There's newspaper accounts and official documents. You can study those."

"Thanks, that'll be of help. But Dr. Walther also indicated there was a question whether Jarred was actually dead. He said some people are convinced he's still alive, and that there've been a series of incidents supporting the belief."

Anna lit her cigarette and blew a cloud of smoke toward the ceiling. "I'll admit this much. There's folks around that are foolish enough to believe Jarred is still wandering the woods like a wild man, killing sheep with his bare hands, stealing food and hunting for virgins by the light of the full moon."

Victoria repressed a smile. When she didn't respond Anna continued. "The rest of us figure that the boy's been dead a long time."

"I guess I know where you stand on the issue." Victoria leaned back in her chair. She knew that prejudices and desires always colored the way people interpreted facts, and Anna Norton was no exception. For that matter, neither was she. The emotional, more romantic part of her wanted to believe Jarred Wilde had survived alone for all these years. But the social scientist in her wanted factual evidence.

"I understand Jarred was a fugitive from justice," Victoria said. "Is that right?"

"Technically, no," Anna said, taking a long drag on her cigarette. "In the end, the district attorney decided not to bring charges. Of course, by then Jarred had taken off. I'm sure he figured the sheriff was out to get him."

"What, exactly, was he supposed to have done? The professor's account was sketchy."

"It's a long story, but I guess it won't hurt none to tell it. You see, Jarred was always polite and respectful. When he was barely five, his father was killed in Viet Nam. Then his mother died of cancer during his junior year of high school. There weren't any relatives around, and nobody wanted to see him go to a state home, so the basketball coach, Bob Simmons, took him in. Jarred was a star on the team and they were close. He stayed with Bob and his wife until he graduated. That's when the trouble really started."

"What trouble?"

"With Todd Parnell. Jarred was popular. Real nice-looking. The girls all adored him. Todd was a good athlete and fairly good-looking himself. Difference was, Todd came from the family that pretty well ran the town, so he resented Jarred.

"The killer was the fact that they both loved the same girl. Todd had gone with Tracey Emerson most of high school. Then, their senior year, she fell for Jarred. They got pretty serious, and even though Jarred was hoping to go to college, there was talk that they might marry. Tracey's father wasn't real happy about it, partly because he'd rather have seen Tracey marry into the Parnells, partly because he wanted Tracey to finish college first.

"Bottom line was, the two kids were being pressured on a couple of sides. There was even a rumor going around that Tracey was pregnant, but I guess it was only a rumor since she never had a baby. But Todd was determined that if he couldn't have Tracey, Jarred wouldn't, either.

"Some people say Todd and his older brother, Steve, tried to shoot Jarred, just out and out kill him. Their uncle was the sheriff, you see, and the Parnell boys pretty well thought they were above the law. And there's no disputing the fact that Todd did jump Jarred one night when he and Tracey were down at the river. There was a place there where the kids would go to neck. Anyway, Todd and Jarred fought. They had a bloody brawl. In the end, Todd wound up dead."

"How did it happen?"

"That's what folks can't agree on. Tracey said that Todd attacked first and Jarred was just defending himself. Steve claimed he saw the whole thing from where he was hiding, and that Jarred kept hitting Todd when he was down. Steve had a gun and, when he realized his brother might be dead, he came out shooting. Understandably, Jarred hightailed it out of there. He went home, got some gear, took off for the mountains and was never seen again."

"The authorities must have searched for him."

"Oh, you better believe the sheriff spared no effort. The Parnells were calling for blood. But all the charges were dropped on account of Tracey's statement. That didn't keep folks from taking sides, though. Some say the fact that Jarred ran off was proof he was guilty. Others say he knew he didn't have a chance considering it was a Parnell who died. The Emersons got Tracey out of town as fast as they could."

"What a bizarre story."

"Sounds like a soap opera, I know. I can't tell you how it tore this town up. Bob Simmons did everything he could to find the boy. He spent months looking for Jarred, hoping he could tell him it was safe to come back. Never did find a trace of him. After a year, he and his wife moved away. The Parnells turned against Bob and he knew his job was in jeopardy anyway. The whole thing was sad."

"I understand there have been several reports of sightings of Jarred over the years," Victoria said. "Why do you dispute them?"

"I suppose it's mostly because of the sources," Anna said, exhaling smoke. "Todd's brother claims to have tracked Jarred down and gotten into a fight with him, but most people discount that story. Steve drinks pretty heavily and that doesn't give his claims much credence. There've been a few others who say they've seen Jarred at a distance or in the dark, but nothing definite like Steve's story. Enough years have passed that folks believe what they want to believe. Personally, I'd like to see the matter left to die."

Victoria was disappointed. She knew she'd taken a chance driving all the way to Washington. It was even possible that her enthusiasm for the project had clouded her judgment, and that the trip would prove to be a waste of time. But the best way to find out the truth was to talk to everyone who had alleged to have sighted Jarred Wilde.

"Sounds to me like Steve Parnell is the person I should talk to," Victoria said.

Anna stubbed out her cigarette. "If you like ghost stories, I suppose he is." She glanced up at the clock on the wall.

"I probably should be going," Victoria said. "I've taken up a lot of your time."

"I've told you all I know, anyway," Anna said. "One day I suspect Jarred's remains will turn up and then the whole business can finally be put to rest."

"May I ask one more question?" Victoria said. "If this fellow Steve Parnell is right, and Jarred is still alive, what do you think he's like now?"

"He's dead, young lady."

"But if he were alive."

"Those who believe Steve's nonsense make Jarred out to be some kind of a werewolf. Even if I thought he was alive, I wouldn't believe that. No, I imagine he'd have the same good heart he had as a boy."

Victoria picked up her briefcase. "Any idea where I can find Steve?"

"The bar is the most likely place. It's up the street."

Victoria went to the door. "Well, thank you for the help, Mrs. Norton."

"Jarred's gone, it's best for all concerned that he stay that way."

Victoria stepped outside. She looked up and down the deserted street. Two men came out of the bar and climbed into one of the two pickups and drove away.

Succumbing to the desolate mood of the town, Victoria thought about what she was up against—fear, indifference, apathy and suspicion.

Yet what if Jarred were alive? Didn't it matter to anyone that he would have been living isolated and alone, scratching out a meager existence like a beast for fifteen long years? What would he be like? Meeting him would be a scholar's dream come true.

Victoria empathized with him. She was from a small town herself, a rural community at the edge of the Salmon Mountains in Northern California. And like Jarred, she'd been orphaned. But for her the outcome hadn't been tragic. Between the income from the small trust her grandmother had set up, and the money she'd gotten from leasing out the ranch, Victoria had been able to get her degree and make a life for herself.

When she got to her car, she stood for a moment in the cutting wind, her eyes tearing from the cold. The clouds above the mountain ridge were already tinged pink. Daylight wouldn't last much longer. The question was whether she should find a motel now or look for Steve Parnell first. Since the bar was just across the street, she decided she might as well go in and inquire about him.

Victoria hadn't spent much time in bars, and she wasn't exactly thrilled about the thought of going into one alone, but the prospect didn't intimidate her, either. It wasn't until she got to the entrance that she noticed the place was called the Bigfoot Saloon. A smile on her face, Victoria stepped inside.

It was dark enough that it took a moment or two for her eyes to adjust. The place was practically empty. A man sporting a shaggy beard stood behind the small wooden bar, large enough for only half a dozen stools, only one of which was occupied.

The mirror behind the bar was circled with Christmas lights—most likely left up all year. Some Bigfoot T-shirts were hanging on the back wall. There were six tables, and a stove against the wall opposite the bar.

Both the lone customer and the bartender looked at her with vacant curiosity. She ambled over to the bar, put her briefcase down and sat on the stool closest to the door.

"Afternoon," the bartender said, moving to where she sat. He was younger than he had at first appeared, probably thirty or thirty-five, and very large.

"Hi," she replied, glancing down the bar at the customer, who was more like fifty.

"What'll you have?"

"Actually I'm looking for someone. Steve Parnell."

"He was here a few minutes ago. You just missed him."

Victoria figured he must have been one of the two men she'd seen leaving in the pickup. "Bad luck," she said.

"Steve might be back later, if you want to wait for him. Could be a couple of hours, though."

She shook her head. "No, don't have the time."

The bartender waited, looking her over. "Want something to drink?" he asked, seeing she wasn't going to leave right away.

"Yeah, maybe a cola."

"That all?"

"Yes."

"One cola, comin' up." He returned with an empty glass into which he slowly poured the soft drink. "You in town just to see Steve?" he asked amiably.

"No, I just heard he might be the guy to talk to."

The man smiled. "I'm sure he'd be pleased to hear that."

"I understand he has some strong opinions about Jarred Wilde. That's the reason I want to talk to him."

The bartender glanced down at the man at the end of the bar, who grinned as he sipped his beer. "Jack, would you say Steve's got strong opinions about Jarred?"

The customer chuckled. "No bull."

"Most people have opinions about Jarred," the bartender said, "if opinions are all you're interested in."

"Did you know Jarred?"

He scratched his beard. "Me and Jarred played basketball together in high school one year, so I knew him pretty well. He was an all-right kid. I liked him."

"What do you think's happened to him?"

The bartender thought for a moment. "I'm sort of on the fence. Most people are generally pretty quick to dismiss the things Steve Parnell says, but personally I don't think he's got a reason to lie about seeing Jarred."

"Booze is all the reason Steve needs," the customer said.

"He tells the same story sober or drunk, Jack."

"Yeah, but was he sober when he supposedly seen him?"

Victoria turned to the man. "I take it you're a nonbeliever."

"After fifteen years, Jarred Wilde is pushing up daisies, sure. If that's bein' a nonbeliever, then, yes, I am."

Victoria took a sip of her drink. "Sounds like I should talk to Steve."

"If you want it from the horse's mouth, he'd be the one to see," the bartender agreed. "Steve ain't shy about givin' his views, especially on Jarred."

"Do *you* think Jarred meant to kill Todd Parnell?"

"I don't know what to think. But Steve's convinced it was murder, I am sure of that." The bartender paused for a moment, as if carefully considering his next words. "For a while, I thought Steve was lying, but it's hard to believe he could keep his anger all this time if it was a made-up story. And it don't make sense to me a guy would go chasing a ghost for fifteen years."

"It's all bull, plain and simple," the man at the far end of the bar said. He sipped his beer as Victoria and the bartender looked at him.

The bartender grinned. "Folks around here don't agree, as you can see."

"Obviously," Victoria said. "Suppose Jarred really is out there, living in the wilds. Do you think he's turned into some kind of animal?"

"Seems he'd have to, if he was to survive. He's probably stark raving mad by now. Imagine not having a conversation with another human being in fifteen years. If he's alive, he's bananas, sure."

"He would be interesting to talk to, though," Victoria said. "No doubt about that."

"If you believe that crock Steve Parnell's spreading, miss, I've got a piece of land I'd like to show you," the customer said with a laugh. "It's priced real cheap."

She turned to the bartender. "Have any idea where Steve Parnell was headed?"

"For home, most likely. I think Tom was droppin' him off."

"Where does he live?" she asked.

"About a mile east of town. Nice modern cabin. It's in a stand of pine on the right side of the road. You can't miss it."

She gestured toward her empty glass. "How much do I owe you?"

"A buck."

Victoria pulled some loose bills from her pocket and laid two dollars on the bar. "Thanks." She readied herself to go back out into the cold.

"You don't plan to go lookin' for Jarred, do you, miss?" the customer asked.

"Maybe. Why?"

"By your questions, I figured you was a reporter or something and you were planning on trackin' him down."

"I'm not a reporter, but I am interested in the story."

The man gazed into his glass of beer. "Don't tell Parnell I said this, but he'll tell you Jarred Wilde wants himself a woman real bad." The man grinned. "Truth is, Steve's the one who's horny. I'd watch myself if I was you."

"Don't talk that way, Jack," the bartender said. "You'll scare the lady."

Victoria picked up her briefcase and smiled. "Thanks, but I don't scare easily. I appreciate the warning, though." With that, she turned and left the bar.

2

STEVE PARNELL'S CABIN was right where the bartender had said she would find it. As Victoria made her way along the driveway to the front of the house, evening was rapidly approaching. She parked next to the Jeep sitting out front. Seeing a light on inside, she figured Steve was inside.

She climbed the steps to the porch and was reaching for the screen door when the main one was opened by a man of thirty-five or so. He was tall and well-built, with blond, shaggy hair and a couple of days' growth of dark beard. He was wearing jeans, a flannel shirt and was in his stocking feet. He had a can of beer in one hand as he looked her over.

"Mr. Parnell?"

"That's me."

"My name's Victoria Ross. I was wondering if we might talk."

"What about?"

"Jarred Wilde."

His expression went from surprise to suspicion, and finally to amusement. He gave her a lazy grin, his eyes skittering down her. "Well, that's a relief. For a minute there I thought you were the new Tupperware lady."

"Afraid not."

"Well, come on in out of the cold." He stepped back and Victoria went in.

She had her guard up, remembering the cautionary words of the man in the bar. But she pretty well had Steve Parnell pegged. She'd known dozens of cowboys like him—the type that started strutting and flexing at the first sight of a woman. They were usually harmless, but nothing could ever be taken for granted, so she'd take it real slow.

She looked around the sparsely furnished cabin. The place was badly in need of a vacuuming and dusting. There was not much in the living room besides a vinyl couch and chair, a TV, a side table and lamp. A pair of boots were sitting in front of the chair, newspapers and a sheepskin jacket were strewn across the couch.

Parnell closed the door and, seeing her surveying the mess, said, "Forgive my housekeeping. I'm still adjusting to bachelor life. The wife and I called it quits a year ago."

"Sorry to barge in on you like this," she said, turning to him. "I know it's not very polite."

As Parnell checked her out, Victoria returned his gaze, unperturbed. Her grandmother had claimed that dealing with a man was not a lot different than dealing with a bear—if you looked them in the eye, they'd back down more often than not.

"No problem," Parnell said, going to the couch. He cleared it. "Take off your coat and make yourself at home."

She wasn't prepared to make herself too comfortable, so she just unzipped her parka. She gave him a businesslike, no-nonsense look. "I won't take much of your time. I'd just like to ask you a few questions about Jarred Wilde."

Then she explained her relationship with Dr. Walther and the fact that she was doing a follow-up to his research.

"Yeah, I talked to him," Parnell said, nodding. "Seemed to me he was more into fairy tales than finding out the truth about Wilde."

"My interests are a little different, Mr. Parnell."

He smiled, taking her in with a sweep of his eye. "Call me Steve . . . and what did you say your name was?"

"Victoria."

"Oh, yes . . . Victoria. Well, let me tell you this, Vicky, if it's Jarred Wilde you want to know about, you came to the right place. I'm the only one who's seen him up close . . . really close . . . in fifteen years. I can tell you about him, leastwise better than anybody else."

Steve Parnell's voice had a ring of sincerity about it— at least that's what she thought she heard. If he were a fraud, she figured it would become clear soon enough. "Good," she said. "Tell me about your last encounter with Jarred, would you?"

He stared at her thoughtfully. "Well, yeah, I can, but it wouldn't hurt if we kind of got acquainted a little. I mean, you just kind of walked in here out of nowhere."

"I'm sorry. I didn't mean to be pushy."

"No problem," he said, waving off her apology. He lifted the can of beer in his hand. "As you can see, I'm having myself a beer. Can I offer you one?"

"No, thank you. I don't drink."

"Not at all?"

"Well, definitely not when I'm working. And I consider this inquiry to be work."

"People have to be social, though. Especially if they come around wanting help." He gave her a lazy smile.

"If you'd prefer, I'll be glad to make an appointment with you. I expect to be in town for several days."

He laughed. "Hey, I'm not playing hard to get. Just the opposite. I'm trying to make you feel at home. If you don't want booze, there must be something you'd like."

"How about a glass of water?"

"With ice cubes and a splash of bourbon?"

"Just ice."

"All right," he said heading off for the kitchen. "A glass of water with ice."

Victoria surveyed the room. By the look of it, Parnell's wife must have taken most of the furniture. "So you say you're a professor, Vicky?" Parnell said from the kitchen.

"A teaching assistant," she said. "I'm a graduate student, actually. Working on my Ph.D."

"Thought you looked more like a coed than a professor," he said with a laugh. He reappeared in the doorway, a tumbler of water in one hand, his can of beer in the other.

Parnell's hair was damp, slicked back in a quick-fix attempt at the kitchen sink to improve his appearance. He was actually good-looking, though his manner completely turned her off. She wondered if he might just be a little more dangerous than she'd assumed at first.

He handed her the glass, then, grinning, he sat across from her, laying on the charm. It was apparent the wheels were turning in his head. Victoria kept her expression sober. She sipped her water and, when she glanced up at him, Parnell was giving her a funny look.

"This really on the up-and-up, Vicky?" he said. "Some of the boys didn't put you up to this?"

"No, honestly. I have Dr. Walther's research materials in the car, if you don't believe me. And I can show you my faculty I.D."

He shook his head. "No, I figured you were for real, but I had to make sure. My buddies are capable of some pretty wild tricks."

"I'm not here because of any prank."

Parnell sipped his beer. "Too bad, in a way. I wouldn't mind it so much if you were from one of those places that sends out pretty girls to take off their clothes and sing 'Happy Birthday.'"

"Listen," she said, annoyed. "If this isn't a good time for a serious conversation, I can come back tomorrow."

"No, no," he said, holding up his hands. "Just a little joke, that's all."

Parnell's expression turned sober and she decided to give it another try. "I understand you tracked Jarred down and got into some kind of fight with him. Are you sure it was Jarred Wilde?"

He chuckled. "Well, the bastard had his fingers around my neck and damned near choked me to death. A person tends to remember a face when they're in the middle of a life-and-death struggle."

"What did he look like?" she asked.

"Well, he had a long beard and he was wearing animal skins. Like a damned caveman. He jumped me when I was climbing some rocks. I looked him right in the eye. There was no doubt in my mind who he was."

"Describe the circumstances, Steve. How did you find him?"

He took a long pull on his beer before he began. "There was a hayride the chamber of commerce put on up by Hayden Lake. After dark some of the couples sort of went off in the moonlight, if you know what I mean. This friend of mine, Willy Jordan, and his girl were in a compromising position. When they looked up and saw Wilde sitting on a boulder watching, it damn near scared the crap out of them, pardon my French. A lot of people thought they were seeing a bear or a tramp or something. But Willy knew Wilde and said it was him.

"Anyway, the next day, three of us borrowed old Jake Cobb's bear hounds and took them up to the lake. They got on Jarred's scent and he proceeded to lead us on a hell of a jaunt. The way he moved up creeks, I knew we weren't on the trail of any bear. He was traveling like a guy who knew there'd be dogs on his butt.

"We went through some rough country, places nobody had likely been before. The other two guys wanted to turn back, but I was determined, so I kept the dogs and pressed on. The scent led up along this escarpment on a high ridge. The dogs had gotten so far ahead of me that I couldn't hear them. Thing is, Wilde killed them. At least we never saw them again.

"Anyway, I'm alone up there and the light's failing fast. I didn't know whether to stop or not. I decided to go for it. When I got to the ridge, I came walking around this boulder and there he was."

Victoria's heart was pounding as she listened to the tale. Steve Parnell could tell a story. But the funny thing was, she didn't find herself sympathizing with him at all. It was Jarred Wilde, a poor creature hunted by his enemies, whom she felt for. "So then what happened?"

"Wilde was on me so fast I didn't know what hit me," he said. "It was like being jumped by a mountain lion. He had me by the throat. I remember looking into his eyes. They were wild and savage-like. His beard was scraggly and his hair long. He scared the hell out of me, I'll tell you that."

"Do you think he meant to hurt you?"

"Well, he wasn't askin' me for a dance. The whole thing happened so fast I only have this flash impression. Boom, he pops up out of nowhere. Boom, he's got me, and the next thing I know I'm going off this cliff."

"A cliff?"

"Actually, I landed on a ledge. The drop was far enough I was knocked unconscious. I don't know if Wilde figured I fell to my death or if he was content to let me be, live or die. In any case, it was the middle of the night before I came to. I was laying right on the edge of a hundred-foot drop, afraid to move a muscle. Worst night of my entire life, bar none.

"Fortunately, my back wasn't broke," he went on, "otherwise I'd have died right there. That was probably what Wilde was countin' on. But all I had was a concussion and a bunch of bruises. Took me two days to walk out of there, though."

"Presumably, when you told everyone what happened, they believed you," Victoria said, testing his reaction.

"The ones that already believed Wilde was out there believed my story. The ones that are sure he died years ago didn't."

"Are you saying the matter ended there?"

"No. After I had a couple of days to recover, a deputy and a group of us went lookin' for Wilde, but we never found a trace of him. No lair, no footprints, not even a scent that could be followed. Naturally, people started discounting my story. But I was there. I looked into the bastard's eyes. His hands were around my neck. I know it was him."

"Is that the only incident involving Jarred?" she asked, inclined to believe him.

"Other people have seen him at a distance, or saw somebody they thought was him. The Wilde sightings run a little ahead of the Bigfoot sightings and are given about the same credence by people who weren't there."

"Has there been anything more recent?"

"This past summer a group of girls from over in Clovis were up at some little fishin' lake in the high country. They said they saw him. Guess he was lurking in the darkness while they were around their campfire. Scared the you-know-what out of them. A couple of 'em went off to pee or somethin' and they said they saw this guy with a hairy face wearing skins. At first they were saying it was Bigfoot, but I know it was Wilde."

"You really think he's survived in the woods for all these years?"

"I'm positive. And don't think I don't go lookin' for him every chance I get. One of these days I'm going to be dragging his carcass back with me, too."

Victoria shivered. She looked into Steve Parnell's eyes, seeing the hatred there. It was impossible for her to summon any sympathy for him. He was the hunter, not the hunted. "Maybe Jarred would come in of his own accord if somebody would give him half a chance," she said. "Has anybody tried reaching out to him?"

Parnell laughed and took a swig of beer. "You sound like a social worker, Vicky. Wilde was a killer before, and now he's a savage."

"He hasn't hurt anyone since he's been in the wilds, has he?"

"It's only a matter of time," Parnell replied. "The way I figure it, he's getting more brazen. I think that business with those girls was a turning point. He's got to have women on the brain. Imagine living like a hermit for fifteen years. Maybe he sees a couple screwing in the woods, or a bunch of girls skinny-dipping. Don't you think that's got to do something to him? Think how long it's been since he's had his hands on a nice sweet . . . well . . . I guess I don't have to spell it out. You know what I mean."

Victoria was silent. The fellow in the bar had told her he would say these things. Obviously, he knew Parnell well. And he'd also told her to be careful. But she was certain she was on to something. Steve Parnell might not be the nicest person, but in her best judgment he wasn't a liar. He leaned back in his chair, looking smug and self-satisfied.

Victoria was getting warm, so she slipped her jacket off, laying it across her knees. Parnell checked out her sweater in an obvious way, which annoyed her, but she didn't say anything. If he was a jerk, there wasn't a lot she could do about it except keep her distance.

"Are you planning to write a book about Wilde?" Parnell asked.

"I might."

"You're pretty serious about researching Wilde, aren't you?" Parnell said, drawing on his beer.

"Yes, I am. I wouldn't be here otherwise."

"I suppose what you'd really like to do is sit down and have a chat with him. Isn't that right?"

Victoria's pulse rate rose. "Yes, that would be ideal— an anthropologist's dream."

He tilted back his head, finishing his beer. "What would you say if I told you I knew how it could be done?"

She looked at him expectantly. Was Parnell playing games with her? Leading her on? "I'd be interested, of course."

He got up and sauntered toward the kitchen. "I'm getting another beer. Like one?"

"No, thanks."

He had left the room for dramatic effect. Victoria was sure of it. Maybe he'd sensed how eager she was and wanted to play with her, it was difficult to tell.

She glanced out the window at the fading light. It would be night soon and she hadn't even begun to think about dinner, let alone where she'd stay. There didn't seem to be any motels in Edgar. She'd probably have to drive halfway to the interstate to find decent lodging. That meant she'd have to get going.

Parnell returned, plopping down in his chair. He drew on his beer and gave her one of those meaningful looks that was long on suggestion but short on specific intent.

"Explain what you mean about knowing how I could talk to Jarred," she said.

He put his beer down on the floor next to his chair and leaned back, his hands behind his head. "It's simple, really. Wilde's proven he's a match for men with guns and dogs, but he's never been tested by a woman. The few who've seen him have run off screaming. I bet he'd love it if some firm little piece like you went into the woods after him, offering to be pals." He grinned smugly.

"In other words, you're suggesting I lure him sexually."

"I don't know that you'd have to strip down naked, but at this point the guy would have to be a sucker for a pretty face. Imagine what it must be like for him."

"Okay, I understand the theory. Maybe Jarred would be more trusting of a woman, and let his guard down. But how do I find him? I wouldn't know where to start looking."

"That's where I come in, honey. I know his hunting ground and I know how to get his attention. It would be up to you to do the rest."

"Why do I feel you aren't suggesting this out of the kindness of your heart? What's your angle?"

Parnell picked up his beer again and took a long drink. "No angle."

"Sorry, I don't buy it. You've been hunting Jarred for years and suddenly you're content just to help me get close enough to interview him? No way."

"Hey, whose side are you on? You don't even know the bastard, and here *I* am, offering my help, and you're calling me a liar."

"I'm not calling you a liar, Steve. I just want to make it clear I won't agree to lure Jarred out into the open just so you can kill him!"

"Vicky, honey, there's got to be something in it for me. This sociological phenomenon of yours killed my brother!"

"We can end this conversation right now if you think I'm going to be your stalking-horse."

His expression turned hostile as he rubbed his stubbly chin. "Maybe I should get myself another girl for the job. Considering how long it's been since Jarred's had a piece, she could probably be a dog and he wouldn't care."

"You intended to use me from the start," she snapped. "I don't know what kind of fool you take me for."

"To hear you, you'd think Wilde was a lost puppy. The sonovabitch is an animal, Vicky."

"You and people like you are the reason he's still out there," she shot back. Getting to her feet, she put on her jacket.

"Wait a minute," he said, lifting his hand. "Don't get all excited."

"Excited? You insult my intelligence by trying to use me, and then you tell me not to get excited? Steve, you no more want to help me than the man in the moon."

"I want this business cleared up, once and for all. I won't rest until my brother's murderer is brought to justice," he replied.

"Didn't it occur to you that could be done without killing the man?"

"What would you do? Sweet-talk him into turning himself in?"

"No one has said a kind word to him in fifteen years. There's no telling what he might do if somebody made an effort to reach out to him."

Parnell fingered his beer can, studying her. "All right, suppose we go out there and talk to him real nice. What if he doesn't cooperate? What if he tries to kill us?"

"There's no reason to think he would. He isn't a predator. He hasn't been stalking and killing people, has he? You're the only one he's fought with, and you were trying to hunt him down."

"Yeah," Steve said sarcastically. "He jumped me in self-defense."

Victoria stared at the man she didn't truly trust. But if she were ever to find Jarred Wilde, she needed his assistance. She sat down again. "So where are we?"

"Right where we started, I guess."

"No, that's not true. If you can get me within sight of Jarred, I think I can communicate with him. The only question is if you're willing to be civilized about this and not act like a mad vigilante."

He scowled.

"So what's the deal?" he said.

"I'm willing to go with you to find Jarred, but under certain conditions."

"Like what?"

"Like I'm in charge. This is a delicate undertaking, psychologically. I think I have a good idea how to approach Jarred. Your job is to get me into his neighborhood. There'll be no guns and no alcohol. We do this seriously and professionally, or we don't do it at all."

"You college types think you've got a monopoly on brains, don't you?"

"You've had fifteen years to find him, Steve. The results haven't been too impressive."

"I've come a helluva lot closer than anybody else."

"Well, maybe it's time to give a college type a try."

He smirked at her, not looking terribly impressed. "If you're planning on doing it this year, Vicky, you don't have much time. The first big winter storm is forming up in the Gulf of Alaska. Soon the high country will be snowed in until spring. As a matter of fact, I was considering making my last run at him in the next day or two."

"You mean we'd have to go right away?"

"I figure we've got two or three days at the most. Wilde probably smells that snow coming and figures he's just about safe for another winter. If he sees you, he might be a little more careless than he otherwise would."

"You men really do think with your gonads, don't you?"

"I know what it would be like to be in his shoes," he said wryly. "Let me put it that way."

Victoria pondered the situation. "You're saying we'd have to leave tomorrow."

"At the crack of dawn, if you want any time up there before the snow hits."

"I don't have my backpacking gear with me."

"I've got plenty of equipment," he said. "All you need are clothes."

Victoria took stock of what was happening. What had been a spur-of-the-moment idea suddenly had become a serious plan. Steve Parnell was suggesting they go off together into the wilderness to track down the Edgar wild man. Did she really know what she was doing, agreeing to go with him?

"Just so we understand each other," she said. "This is a serious business. There'll be no fooling around. If you've got any ideas, you might as well know I'm handy with a gelding knife—hundreds of steers have discovered what I can do when I mean business."

He laughed. "Hey, you're a real firecracker, aren't you?"

"No, Steve, I'm dead serious."

He contemplated her. "There's one thing, though. I'm not going up into the high country without a rifle. I'll agree to no booze, but a man's got to be armed. Wilde's not the only danger."

"All right, but I want your word you won't use it on Jarred. Under any circumstances."

He begrudgingly nodded his head. "You're a hard boss, honey."

"I don't want any misunderstandings."

"You got a place to stay for the night?"

"I figured I'd find a motel."

"There's nothing decent within fifty miles. You can bunk here. I've got a spare bedroom."

She shook her head. "I'll borrow a sleeping bag and stay in my car."

"You're going into the woods with me, but you won't sleep in my house?" he said incredulously.

"You're already half-drunk. In the woods there'll be no booze. Besides, the cold mountain air will be sobering."

He smiled. "You got it all figured out, don't you?"

"With a guy as bright as you," she said, "a woman's got to stay on her toes."

"I've got some hamburger in the fridge. How about if I make you dinner? That wouldn't offend your sensibilities, would it?"

"That would be fine," she said.

Parnell nodded, a grin spreading over his face. "You know, Vicky, I've got a feeling you and me will make a good team."

She looked him dead in the eye. "There's one other thing. My name is *Victoria*."

3

VICTORIA SPENT the night worrying about her decision to go into the woods with Steve Parnell. But something in her gut told her their plan just might work. And the prospect of actually coming face-to-face with Jarred Wilde, a man who'd been cut off from civilization for a decade and a half, was incredibly exciting.

What would Jarred's state of mind be after so many years of living alone? Would he be paranoid and deeply disturbed, or simply alienated from the world in which he had grown up? Surely he was strong. No human being could endure such isolation without formidable inner strength. But how would he react to her, the first female he'd encountered in years? That was the most intriguing question of all.

Victoria slept far better than she'd expected. She didn't wake until Parnell began scratching the frost off the rear window of her car.

"Up and at 'em, honey," he called through the glass. "Coffee's on, and it's time to go huntin'."

Seeing white vapors spewing from his grinning mouth, Victoria had a sudden premonition that in agreeing to go with him, she had made a dangerous commitment.

"I'll be with you in a minute," she called through the glass, waving to let him know she was awake.

"I'm going back inside," Parnell said. "Front door will be unlocked."

Victoria nodded and dropped her head back down on the seat. By the light of day things always looked different than they did at night, when one's instinct for romance and adventure was at its peak. She had gotten carried away—no question about it. Steve Parnell, on the other hand, didn't seem to have lost his taste for the enterprise. Even sobriety hadn't changed his mind.

She had slept in her clothes, so she didn't need to dress, although she wanted to go to the bathroom. She would have a cup of coffee with Parnell, then reassess the situation.

Clambering to the door, she found the smell of food welcome. Dropping the sleeping bag on the floor, she went to the kitchen. Parnell was standing at the stove with a skillet in his hand. He glanced over his shoulder at her and smiled.

"Good morning, *Victoria*," he said, making a point of her name. "Ready to soothe the savage beast?"

"You still plan to go through with this?" she asked.

"Don't tell me you're getting cold feet."

"Not exactly, but I figured you might have thought better of it."

"Why, because I had a few beers in me?"

"Maybe."

"Actually, the idea sounds even better now than it did last night. I think my plan just might work."

He'd shaved and was bright-eyed. There did seem to be a somewhat more good-natured air about him. She'd either seen him at his worst the night before, or he was putting on a hell of an act now. Her skepticism told her to be cautious, whatever the truth.

"How do you like your eggs?" he asked.

"Usually after my shower."

"Can't you eat first? Breakfast is practically ready."

"All right, but I'm going to the bathroom right now. Some things are not negotiable."

Everything was on the table by the time she returned. Parnell was not a changed man, but he was a good deal more agreeable when he was sober.

"Tell me the truth," she said, leaning back with her coffee mug in hand. "Are you doing this because of Jarred, or because of me?"

He rubbed his clean-shaven chin. "You're askin' if I plan to hit on you."

"You might put it that way."

"I'll admit the thought crossed my mind. I appreciate a sweet little piece as much as the next guy, but, to tell you the truth, I'm even more obsessed with Wilde. If you've got the guts to do this, then I sure as hell do."

"I came in here wondering if this was really such a good idea," she said. "I'm glad to see you're being levelheaded about it."

"You can be a very persuasive lady, Victoria."

In spite of his attempt at friendliness, she wasn't fool enough to think a skunk could change his stripes. Still, if Parnell stayed away from alcohol, he'd probably remain reasonable long enough for her to get a chance to contact the wild man. That was really all she needed. "Tell me," she said. "How are we going to get close enough for me to talk to Jarred?"

"He knows how to get close. He's proven that already. And I think you're all the incentive he'll need," Parnell said with a leer. He got the coffeepot, pouring them each some more.

Victoria sensed he was being a tad too compliant and felt uneasy again about trusting him. "Maybe it's a mistake for just the two of us to go," she said, curious how he'd respond. "Some help wouldn't hurt, would it?"

"A posse would never get close to him. I even have doubts he'll come near you with me along, but there's no way you can go in alone. Besides, I want to be the one who brings him out—and if it has to be alive, then so be it."

"That's my condition for going through with this."

Parnell sipped his coffee. "Yeah, I know. We're doing it the college way."

"The sensible way," she corrected.

He didn't argue, but he didn't look convinced, either. "Well, time's a wastin'. Shall we have a look at the gear?"

THEY WENT much farther in the Jeep than Victoria had thought was possible. The trailhead was well up in the high country and Parnell hoped to reach the site where Jarred would be able to sight them on the first day.

"Most likely, Wilde will observe us for a night to get a handle on the situation," Parnell said, as he opened the back of the Jeep. "I don't expect anything to happen until tomorrow."

Victoria watched him remove his rifle from the leather case and insert a round in the chamber. "That gun won't signal that our intentions are friendly," she said, vapors from her mouth dissipating in the icy air.

"My intentions aren't," he said. "Only yours are." He held up his hand before she could protest. "I know, I promised not to shoot the bastard. And I'll keep my word. But if it's a matter of self-defense, I won't let him take me. Or you, either."

Her doubts about Parnell's intentions returned. She sensed he'd lied, that his promise not to hurt Jarred was empty. It wasn't too late to turn back, but then she thought of Jarred. This was her one opportunity to come face-to-face with him, the chance of a lifetime. If Parnell did get out of line, she'd simply call a halt to the operation—even if it meant walking all the way back to town by herself.

Feeling somewhat better, but still apprehensive, Victoria helped unload the gear. Then Parnell locked the Jeep and they headed up the trail with him in the lead. The ground was frozen, and lightly covered with snow.

Parnell moved at a steady gait and Victoria fell into rhythm behind him. The trail angled up a rocky slope dotted with pines. The saddle at the top, a couple of thousand feet above them, was at the foot of a high mountain valley where Parnell figured that Jarred would be foraging for his winter stores. The spot was in the center of the area in which most of the Wilde sightings had occurred. The ridge where the two men had fought was on one side of the valley, and was in all probability near Jarred's lair.

Parnell had gone over topographic maps of the area in fine detail, concluding the mountains on either side of the high valley afforded the best refuge. He told Victoria that in the past he'd walked each ridge line at least twice without turning up anything. That proved nothing really, since there were a million crooks and crannies in which a man could hide.

"My bet is he has two or three hiding places so that if one is compromised he'll have another," Parnell had informed her on the drive up. "Given the season, he's likely living in his primary lair. The odds are good he'll be out and moving about because there are very few people in the mountains this time of year."

After thirty minutes of climbing, Parnell called a rest stop. Victoria propped herself against a boulder so as to ease the weight of the backpack off her shoulders. She was breathing heavily and the icy air felt like fire in her lungs. Still, she was perspiring and took off her cap to cool her head.

Parnell also had on a stocking cap, but wore a sheepskin coat instead of a parka. He, too, was breathing deeply as he looked at her.

"I love the outdoors," he said, grinning. "But fifteen years of this in one chunk is a bit more than I'd care for."

"Jarred's got to be remarkable. Imagine living out here alone." She scanned the slope and then peered down into the trees in the gorge below them. Almost from the start she had been watching for something, expecting to see a shadowy figure darting behind a tree or clambering over rocks. Though a sighting should have been welcome, the thought of it sent a shiver up her spine. She was disposed to think the best of Jarred, but she couldn't truly be sure what he would be like now.

"Wilde's no shrinking violet," Parnell said, "but I got a theory I haven't told anybody about."

"What's that?"

He turned and looked at her. "I think he gets help from somebody. Nothing major, probably, but supplies now and then."

"From whom?"

"I haven't figured that out yet. But the way I see it, he'd need some things from time to time. It'd be damned hard to impossible to live completely off the land for years at a time."

Victoria didn't know what to make of the comment. Parnell had obviously been obsessing about Jarred Wilde for years.

"Well," he said, the spirit of adventure showing in his voice. "You ready for another run at the top?"

"Yeah, let's go."

They took off again, climbing more steeply now. Whenever the woods got dense, Victoria's apprehension rose. Once she saw motion on a mound of boulders nearby. She gasped, but it was only a well-fattened muskrat scurrying for cover. The deer had probably already moved to lower ground, and the mountain lions with them. The only larger animals they were likely to see would be bear.

They stopped twice more, though only briefly. Soon after starting again, Victoria heard the sound of rushing water. "Is there a falls up ahead?" she asked.

"Yes," Parnell said, stopping to catch his breath. "A pretty fair sized one flowing into the gorge."

Another ten minutes of climbing and they were quite near the falls. Victoria had to use her hands to help her move along the rugged trail. Soon they came to an open space where they could see the falls. The cascading water was illuminated by the late-morning sun.

"What a breathtaking view," Victoria remarked.

"It's nice country," Parnell agreed. "I hope Wilde's into scenery because that's about all he's had to look at for the last fifteen years." He whooped with laughter and Victoria gave him a disapproving look. "Come on, Vicky," he said, frowning. "Lighten up."

Just then they heard a ferocious roar. Filled with terror, Victoria spun around. A huge black bear reared up on its hind legs, not a hundred feet away from them. As Parnell lifted his rifle to his shoulder, Victoria spotted a pair of cubs scampering up a nearby tree.

"Don't shoot! It's a she-bear with cubs," she whispered. "Let's get out of here."

They slowly backed away, expecting the bear to charge at any moment. Luckily, she didn't. Once they'd made it into a wooded area out of sight of the bears, Victoria sat down on a log to calm herself. Her heart was still pounding.

"My God," she said. "I haven't been that close to a wild animal in years."

"Yeah, well picture that bear pouncing on you. That's the way it was when Wilde jumped me."

"You make him sound like he's ten feet tall. He's only a man, Steve."

"He's a beast, honey. And before this is over, you'll be agreeing with me. All your sociology crap sounds nice, but if Wilde is as eager to get in your pants as I think he is, you'll be damned glad I've brought this rifle along."

"Has it ever occurred to you that Jarred might not be as single-minded about sex as you are, Steve?"

He gave her a hard contemptuous look. "Maybe you better hope you won't get to find out, *Vicky*."

She let the matter drop, definitely not liking the direction of their conversation. After waiting ten minutes to give the bears time to move on, they resumed their climb. The terrain was getting rougher and Victoria was glad she'd had a lot of experience in the outdoors. Before long they'd made it to the valley floor where they took another breather.

The edge of the stream was crusted with snow, and the water moved at a more tranquil pace than it had in the gorge. The ground was frozen solid in all but the open areas where the sun could warm it. Resuming their trek, they ambled at a leisurely gait, the weight on their backs not nearly so onerous as during the climb.

"I figure we camp here in the valley," Parnell said. "A mile or so upstream there's a meadow. If you get out in the middle of it, Wilde will be able to see you from just about anywhere on the surrounding ridges. I don't know how good his eyesight is, but the way I figure it, if he has any inkling you're a woman, he'll come running."

The notion that Steve Parnell might be right made her edgy. In the living room of his cabin, she'd been much more confident of her ability to deal with Jarred Wilde. Out here in the wilds, her confidence waned.

Maybe she was overreacting. Jarred was, after all, a human being. He hadn't always lived in the wilderness. He'd finished high school. He'd had a serious relationship with a girl. He'd been young when he'd taken refuge in the mountains, it was true, but old enough to have considered marriage. The problem was he'd left behind a real mess—one that he'd either been too afraid, or too alienated from the community, to face.

"Getting tired?" Parnell asked.

"I'm okay."

He gave her a macho grin. "You're doing better than I expected, if you want to know the truth."

"I told you I'm not a wimp."

"Well, let's see how you do when it gets dark and you know old Wilde is sittin' in the woods, watchin' you."

"You sound like a kid telling scary stories, Steve. There's no point in trying to spook me."

"Don't worry, honey. If you get scared, you can always crawl into my sleeping bag. You'll be safe there." He laughed then, his voice echoing through the woods.

"Knock it off. Remember—we have a deal."

"Yeah, I know. You're the boss. Let's see if you've still got brass balls when all that's between you and the wild man is me and this rifle."

Victoria sighed with exasperation, certain now that she was going to be in for a rough time with Parnell. Thank God, she'd insisted that there be no alcohol. As long as he remained sober, she'd be able to keep him in line. Even so, a tiny part of her wished it wasn't too late to head back to Edgar.

After another twenty minutes of walking they came to the meadow. She had little difficulty walking on the frozen ground. For a moment, she paused to survey the area. Parnell was right. She could walk across it and be seen from the mountains for miles around.

Parnell dropped his pack and stared out at the meadow. "Too damned bad it's not bikini weather," he said. "You could get out there and drive the bastard mad."

"Let's not blow this out of proportion," she said curtly. "For all we know, I'm not Jarred's type."

Parnell laughed. "He's not in much of a position to be choosy."

Victoria shook her head. "You're going to owe both Jarred and me an apology, Steve, when you find out you were wrong about him." She said it with all the conviction she could muster, in spite of her doubts.

"Well, there's no point in debating it now," he said. "Time will tell." He looked around. "What do you say? Shall we pick out a campsite, then bait our trap?"

JARRED SAT with his chin resting in his hands as he stared down at the tiny red figure moving back and forth across the valley floor. He couldn't be certain whether it was a man or a woman. Still, something told him it was a female and that bothered him.

"Damn," he muttered, absently tugging the ends of his beard. He leaned back against the boulder, exasperated. Then he closed his eyes, trying to calm himself as he let the sun warm his face. "What could it mean?" he mumbled out loud. "What are they up to?"

He'd long since spotted the second person, partially hidden in the trees at the edge of the meadow. Every once in a while the sun had reflected off something—a shiny metal cup, a mirror, or maybe the barrel of a rifle—betraying his location. He hadn't spotted any

others. Later on he'd have to scout around some more
to be sure there weren't any.

It was too late in the year for most people to be out
in the woods. The one in the red wasn't picking flow-
ers, so all that pacing back and forth had to be for his
benefit. They were trying to get his attention. That
meant they were hunting for him.

Opening his eyes, he leaned forward again and
peered down from his lookout. Yes, the one in red was
a woman. And he was pretty sure she wanted to make
him curious. The damned trouble was, she was suc-
ceeding.

VICTORIA PACED until she grew fatigued with sheer
boredom. Her performance could turn out to be a total
waste of energy. Jarred Wilde could be off gathering
nuts someplace and not have the vaguest idea she was
even there. Or he might have been mauled by a bear
years before or fallen off a cliff and died.

She meandered to the edge of the meadow where
Parnell sat on a log under the protective canopy of the
forest, his rifle across his knees, watching her.

"Are we having fun yet?" he asked jokingly.

"Very funny," she said. "Do you really think this is
doing any good?"

"I suspect we'll find out soon enough."

"Like when?"

"Tonight maybe," Parnell said. "Don't expect Wilde
to come waltzing in to say howdy. He might be horny
but he's not stupid."

"He'll jump me after dark. Is that what you're suggesting?"

"Without me to protect you, honey, you'd be dog meat before daylight. Trust me."

She shook her head, realizing he was incorrigible. Her real worry was that Parnell was dangerous. If he thought he was going to be able to scare her into his arms, she'd have to straighten him out real quick.

Victoria turned and started back across the open field. "I'll give another hour of this to the cause," she said over her shoulder. "Then I'm through for the day."

JARRED CREPT through the darkness, his heart beating wildly. It was always like this when he got close to people, the sight of them evoking memories of the disappointments he'd had, the resentment that never seemed to go away. And yet when an opportunity came along, he was drawn to them.

The acrid scent of wood smoke was strong. They had built a fire, though he couldn't yet see it. He would, soon enough. In the woods, nobody even came close to being a match for him. That gave him confidence when, by all rights, he should have been afraid.

He was almost certain that there were only two of them. When he'd checked the trail farther down the valley, he'd discovered only two sets of tracks. One set was small, confirming that one was a woman. If the other set belonged to Parnell, it meant he'd started using bait.

Jarred moved forward again, carefully making his way through the woods. He was approaching from downwind. It was not an important tactic when stalking people, but men sometimes had dogs, and a good one could pick up his scent in the wind.

He didn't worry about being discovered, especially at night. If he wanted, he could stroll around a campground for hours and not be noticed, even if somebody got up to take a pee.

When he did venture near a campsite, it was because he felt an uncontrollable urge to be near others of his kind. He didn't trust people, yet there was something inside him that wouldn't let him leave them alone, either. Not completely.

He caught sight of the campfire. His pulse quickened and he fingered his beard, wondering if he'd get a good look at the woman. Few of them ventured so high into the mountains, and he was always fascinated whenever he got a chance to be near one. Often he'd watch a group of campers sitting around a fire, laughing and talking. He was wary of them, even the children, but their voices were like music, a song for his ears.

Once, many years ago, he'd gotten one of those terrible aching lonely feelings. It had been so bad he'd seriously considered going back, just for the human contact, even if it meant getting thrown in jail. Instead, he'd trekked down to a campground a mile off the highway, a place where he knew there'd be people. He got there before dark, biding his time, listening to the human voices and noises echoing through the woods.

There had been two or three large families together. When one of the men got out a guitar and they all started to sing, Jarred crept closer, so close he could smell the bubble gum and perfume and kerosene from the lanterns. He wasn't more than ten yards from them as they sang the songs that he had known as a boy. It had brought tears to his eyes, and he hated it that he couldn't walk right in to the fire ring and sit down. He'd closed his eyes and mouthed the words along with the singers.

Whenever he thought of that night, he could hear their voices as if it were happening all over again.

He rarely ventured near campgrounds after that, unless he was certain everyone was asleep. It was enough to share their space, to touch their gear, to sit down alone by the glowing coals.

This was different than that time. It was different from all the other times, too. This pair—the man and the woman—knew he was out here.

The hunted were always in danger. He knew that. Jarred crept closer to the flames, stopping at the sound of voices. Cocking his head, he listened. One voice was definitely a woman's. But he didn't let his excitement get to him. He had to be smarter, especially if the guy was Steve Parnell. His survival depended on it.

"WELL, I'LL BE DAMNED," Parnell said. "You actually did rodeo? I can see you on a horse, but not a bronc. What do you weigh, a hundred pounds?"

"I weigh enough," Victoria said. "You don't have to be large to fall off a horse."

He laughed and got up from the log to stretch his legs. Victoria was sitting cross-legged on a ground cloth on the opposite side of the fire. Parnell looked down at her and smiled, shadows from the flames dancing on his face.

"If you'll excuse me, Vicky...sorry, *Victoria*, I'll just go into the tent a minute." He grabbed the rifle that was leaning against the log and handed it to her. "Don't fire until you see the whites of his eyes," he said, hooting with laughter. Then he went over and crawled into the small, domed tent.

Victoria let the rifle rest on her knees and stared out beyond the fire. Darkness had settled on the forest like ink into soft paper. The trees encircling the camp were illuminated by the fire. The visible world had shrunk to a very small space, and the darkness seemed immense.

She turned and looked at the tent, curious what Parnell was up to. It was the second time he'd gone inside in the past twenty minutes. Then it struck her he had a flask hidden in his pack.

"Steve," she said, her voice accusing. "Do you have a bottle in there?" She drew an angry breath. "Do you?"

His head appeared at the zippered opening of the tent. "Just a few drops to fight the cold and warm the insides a little," he said grinning guiltily. He extended the flask through the opening. "Like a nip?"

"Dammit, you promised there'd be no booze."

"Oh, come on, Vicky, this is practically medicinal. A guy's got to keep his insides warm."

"Steve, we made a deal."

His contrite expression slowly turned to anger. "Don't be so damned prissy. A little drink never hurt anybody. Besides, there's hardly enough here to get high, let alone drunk. And if you have your share, that'll be less for me."

"Nice try."

He crawled out of the tent and stood up, knocking his head back and guzzling the booze defiantly.

"I told you I'd call this off, if you didn't play straight," she said angrily. "I never should have come."

"You might be a teacher," he snapped, "but I'm no schoolboy. If you don't like my company, then why don't you leave?" He dug into his pants pocket and pulled out his car keys, dangling them in his hand. "Here. Take the Jeep."

When her only response was a sullen look, he laughed, put the keys back in his pocket and quaffed some more whiskey.

Victoria got up and went around to the log, keeping the fire between them. Her worst fear had just been realized. She was out in the middle of nowhere with a crazed nut who was showing every indication of intending to get very drunk.

She'd been a fool to let her desire to see Jarred cloud her judgment. It was too late to do anything about it now. At least she was the one with the rifle in her hands. And that could end up being Steve Parnell's mistake.

4

STEVE PARNELL STOOD in the firelight like a satyr, guzzling his whiskey in hostile defiance, leering at her between gulps. He was obviously trying to get drunk as fast as he could.

Victoria realized he was seeking the courage to rape her. She squeezed the stock of the rifle with her gloved hand, remembering what her grandmother had said about staring a man down, the same as a bear. This time, though, the rifle seemed a much more reliable weapon.

Stopping for a breath, Parnell gave her a giddy look. "This stuff does wonders for you in the fresh air," he said, waving the flask. "Sure you don't want to join the party?"

"You're disgusting," she said with revulsion.

"Well, you're a bitch," he snarled, as he drained the last of the alcohol and tossed the flask aside. "Or maybe your problem is that you've never had a real man before."

"Knock it off, Steve. Why don't you get your sleeping bag and roll it out by the fire? Use the ground cloth. It'll be nice and cozy for you."

He was weaving. "You've just got to play teacher, don't you? Can't keep your mouth shut and act like a woman."

Victoria glared.

"Okay," he said grinning stupidly. "I'll get my sleeping bag." He pulled it from the tent and dragged it toward the fire. After a halfhearted attempt to spread out the ground cloth, he put the sleeping bag on it, smoothing the corners ceremoniously. "There. That make you happy, *Vicky?*"

"That's fine. I'm sure you'll be very comfortable."

He grinned again. "I'll be comfortable all right, because you're going to be in here with me. Naked as a jaybird."

She shook her head, narrowing her eyes. "Forget it."

"Don't it sound good to you?"

"Go to bed, Steve."

He got back to his feet and Victoria picked up the rifle so that it lay across her lap. She glared at him.

"Oh, so you plan to shoot me. Is that it?" He started to stumble around the fire, coming toward her.

She stood, lifting the muzzle so that it pointed vaguely in his direction. "I'll do whatever I have to do."

"I think you'd rather get laid," he said, taking another step toward her.

Victoria pointed the rifle square at his chest, bringing him to an abrupt halt. His expression sobered.

"I'm beginning to think you just might pull the trigger," he mumbled.

"You got that right."

His face twisted into a pained expression. "Damn it, Vicky, why do you have to spoil everything? We could have a real high time."

"Steve, go to bed!"

He glanced up at the black sky, his body weaving as he stared at the stars. "God, here we are under this romantic sky. Look up there, Vicky, don't that do anything for you? Don't it make you want it?"

She didn't look up, but his words, his compliant tone, distracted her just enough that she wasn't prepared for him when his left hand flashed out, grabbing the muzzle of the rifle. He jerked it in an attempt to wrench it from her hands and the thing went off, the explosion renting the silence of the night.

For a moment, she thought she'd shot him. When his lips curled over his teeth, she realized that the bullet had gone harmlessly into the woods.

"You might be a cowgirl, honey," he said, "but you ain't no Annie Oakley."

She tried to wrench the weapon away, but he held the barrel firmly.

"It's a single-shot rifle. It won't do you any good now."

Victoria turned to run, but the log she'd been sitting on was closer than she anticipated and she fell over it. Parnell was instantly on her, pulling her back up by the shoulders of her jacket. A scream of pure terror wedged in her throat.

"What...about...Jarred?" she stammered, her voice shaking. "You said he'd be out there. That shot will bring him for sure."

Parnell lifted his brows in mock horror. "Wouldn't that be too bad! Of course, maybe he'd enjoy it. I imagine Wilde could do with a little sex education."

"You wouldn't!"

He clamped his mouth on hers, his teeth sinking into her lips, his sour breath filling her lungs. Victoria wrenched her mouth free.

"I hope he kills you," she spat, wiping her lips with her sleeve.

Parnell laughed. He had her by her jacket. He was strong enough that he practically lifted her off the ground as he yanked her back toward the fire, pausing only to pick up the rifle. When they got to the sleeping bag, he threw her down, putting his booted foot on her stomach to hold her there.

He was going to rape her. Reasoning with him seemed useless, but she had to try. "Jarred will come, Steve, and he'll get us both. Don't be stupid."

Parnell had fished through his pocket for another bullet, which he'd put into the chamber. "Honey, I'm man enough to take care of you and Wilde at the same time." He let the rifle hang in his hand. "Now, do you want to be a good girl and take off your clothes, or are you going to make me take them off for you?"

"I'll kill you first," she replied bitterly. "I swear it."

He laughed and dropped down on one knee beside her, keeping the other on her stomach so she couldn't move. After carefully laying the rifle down behind him, he pulled off her stocking hat, tousling her hair with his fingers. "You know, you're actually a damned good-lookin' broad. You got a real nice mouth. Nice enough I think I'll have me another taste."

As he leaned over to kiss her, Victoria whacked him across the side of the face, stunning him momentarily. Enraged, he hit her hard on the jaw.

"You watch that!" he screamed. "Hear?"

Dazed from the blow, Victoria struggled to free herself. It was no use—he was too strong for her. The next thing she knew he was on top of her, one hand grasping her firmly between the legs.

"No, Steve, don't!" she cried, the tears spouting from her eyes and running down her cheeks.

He moved his hand up under her parka and began fumbling with her belt. His hot, sour breath was on her cheek. "Now you be real sweet, honey, and you might like this a whole lot."

Victoria felt as if she was about to vomit. God, how could this be happening to her?

Parnell got up on his knees then, bringing one firmly up between her legs. He unbuttoned his sheepskin coat, reached down and pulled the zipper of her parka open.

The fire was beginning to die down, deepening the shadows on his face, making him seem even more ominous. She rolled her head to the side, so as not to look at him. The fire ring was just a few feet away, within reach. Her eye fell on a rock about the size of a grapefruit.

Parnell was so fixed on her body that he didn't notice her arm flop out toward the rock. He was unfastening her belt, pausing to run his callused hand up under her sweater. It was then they heard a crash across the campsite, beyond the fire. Parnell jerked his head up abruptly. Victoria lifted herself to her elbows, turning to see what he was looking at. Through the flames she saw him, a bearded monster the size of a bear. He was in skins and fur, a veritable caveman. "Oh, my God," she murmured.

The man-beast had a large branch in his hand that he carried like a club. The fire had burned down enough that he was more a shadowy apparition than a distinct figure.

"Jesus," Parnell said, reaching slowly for the rifle as he got off of her.

Victoria got to her knees, avoiding any abrupt motion.

The beast, his eyes iridescent in the firelight, took a couple of side steps, moving slowly, like a stalking predator. Parnell had the gun in his hands, but hadn't aimed yet.

"Don't shoot, Steve," she whispered.

"What do you want me to do, invite him over?"

"Jarred," she called out with a trembling voice. "We're your friends."

"Fat chance he'll believe that," Parnell said out of the corner of his mouth. "The thing to do is finish him off while I've got a clear shot."

The wild man continued to slip laterally through the brush at the edge of the clearing, just inside the ring of trees, his eyes on them as he circled. Victoria was shaking with fear.

"I'm going to get the sonovabitch," Parnell muttered. He raised the rifle to his shoulder and Victoria lunged for it, pulling it down.

"Don't!"

Turning to her with fury in his eyes, Parnell swung the back of his hand and hit her mouth so hard, she was knocked to the ground. Then he aimed and fired. But it was a hasty shot, striking the tree above the wild man's head.

Parnell reached into his pocket for another bullet, cursing. He was shaking so badly that it took extra seconds to reload. Victoria knew she had to stop him. She grabbed the rock while he was aiming and flung it at his head. As it struck him, the gun went off again.

Parnell fell to the ground, blood oozing from the side of his skull. The rifle was under his body, but it was useless unless she reloaded.

Victoria turned to face the wild man across the clearing. He was barely visible now. The flames from the campfire had died down to the point where they were now little more than blue tongues rising from the coals. The arena grew progressively darker, the light dying even as they stood there, staring at each other.

"Jarred?" she said, her voice sounding feeble in the emptiness of the woods.

He did not say anything, though he took a tentative step toward her. She moaned.

"I'm your friend," she said softly. She glanced down at Steve Parnell. He was motionless. He didn't even seem to be breathing. "Oh, my God," she muttered under her breath.

Victoria felt as if the night were swallowing her up. She panicked. Turning to run she plunged into the forest, running mindlessly, unable to see, intent only on getting away.

She was aware of the black mass of the trees looming up as she ran full tilt. Bushes grabbed her legs. Low branches tore at her face. Victoria imagined the beast in pursuit, roaring hideously like that she-bear. She could almost feel him behind her, his dark claws reaching for her, ready to rip her apart.

Somehow she managed to keep going, fighting her way through the darkness, falling, scrambling to her feet and falling again. Then she came into the open, the stream before her. Without thinking, she plunged into it. Before she made it to the far side, a large rock seemed to rise in front of her like a sea monster, crashing into her head. Her last conscious thought was a vague awareness of her body sinking into the icy arms of death.

THE WIND MOANED eerily in symphonic counterpoint to the persistent, merciless pounding in her head. Victoria shivered under the covers, her body heat inadequate against the unrelenting chill.

Her eyes closed, she listened to her teeth chattering like rhythmless castanets as she drifted into semiconsciousness.

She smelled apples. Her grandmother must be cooking applesauce. Soon Grandmother would bring her a steaming hot bowl of applesauce and a cup of tea to warm her insides. Yes. And aspirin and water for her fever. She was very thirsty. A glass of water would be lovely.

Why did her bed smell so foul, like Scooter? Grandmother never allowed him in the house. He had to stay outside to guard the apple trees against the bear that wandered down from the mountains to forage. Sometimes, though, if the temperature went below freezing, Grandmother would let him in the mud room to sleep with the cat.

Victoria smiled at the thought. Scooter and the cat, sharing a bed. How could that be? Scooter was dead.

The bed couldn't smell like him. And Grandmother... she had died a long, long time ago.

Death. Everybody was dead. Was she dead, too?

She wiggled her toes. No. She couldn't be dead if she could still move them. She raised her right leg. It came up against something hot and very hard—so hot it burned her, made her moan. There was another hot thing behind her back, and on the other side, too.

She struggled to open her eyes, but there was only darkness—moist cool darkness that smelled like apples and earth. She tried to concentrate, her mind plodding along like a blind person in a field of snow. Grandmother's ranch. Berkeley. Her students. Dr. Walther. That little town. The old woman. The bar across the street. Steve Parnell. *Steve Parnell!*

It all came back to her. She remembered her terror, running through the darkness. Being consumed by the icy water. She *was* dead!

Victoria lifted her head, setting off the terrible throbbing pain in her temples. And her jaw, where Parnell had hit her, ached as well.

She slid her hands over her hip, her abdomen and breasts—her clammy, hot, cold, utterly naked body.

Those hot things pressing against her. What were they?

Victoria touched one. It was smooth and very hot. A rock. A hot rock.

She worked her hand to the top of the covers. It wasn't a blanket at all. It was furry, a pelt, an animal skin.

She started, shaking violently, petrified. Where was she? Oh God, why was it so dark?

She was trembling so hard she began to cry. Then *he* came into her mind—just as he had come into the circle of light at the campsite. The wild man. Jarred.

All at once she understood. He'd carried her off. She was in his lair, and she was naked. Her hand slipped over her flesh to her mound. Gingerly she probed to see if she was sore. No pain. No blood. He hadn't raped her. Yet he'd undressed her, touched her. She shivered violently at the thought that he had seen her naked. God, she thought, don't let him be the sex maniac Parnell made him out to be.

Victoria raised her head again, this time with more success. There was a faint light in the distance. She squinted. Rock walls? A cave. Of course, she was in a cave.

Her head dropped back to the makeshift pillow. She turned her head and sniffed. Straw? Leaves? Feathers? Skins? No wonder the bed smelled like a dog.

Where was Jarred? Had he left her to go hunting? Or was he somewhere in the darkness of the cave?

Victoria tried to clear her mind and bring everything into perspective. Jarred had carried her off. He hadn't hurt her—at least not yet. Maybe he wasn't the horrible beast he'd seemed. Maybe she could reason with him.

Was she deluding herself? What would be the best way to handle him? Should she be firm or gentle? And what was it he wanted, anyway? It must have taken considerable effort to get her to this place. Clearly he had something in mind for her, but what?

As she lay agonizing, attempting to suppress her fear, Victoria heard a rustling sound. She held her breath. Was it a rat? A snake? Or was it *him*?

The glow on the far wall seemed to grow brighter. Suddenly a small flame appeared. An arm appeared beneath it, then a shoulder and a head.

It was the wild man and he was half-naked! She watched him rise to nearly his full height once he was in the chamber. He was dragging a blanket or skin that he lifted over his shoulders.

The penlight of flame was in his hand, illuminating only one side of him. She could not see his face, only his hair and beard. He started toward her and she cringed, uncertain what to do. Lying back, she feigned unconsciousness, while sneaking glances at him.

He came closer, extending the light to see her better. For the first time, she could see his face clearly. It was surprisingly serene, a remarkably attractive face. He was no monster, as she'd imagined—despite the full, dark beard and long hair. His eyes were a lovely blue, the color of the sky, his nose straight and even. His was the face of an artist, not a savage. And yet there he stood, naked, except for the animal skin wrapped around him.

He moved closer still and she shut her eyes tightly so that he wouldn't know she was awake. When he stepped onto the edge of her pallet she opened one eye a crack to confirm that he was kneeling over her.

She began shaking as she felt his hand on her face. She tensed, but forced herself not to cry out. He pressed the back of his fingers against her throat and cheek as though he were a doctor, or a loving father tending to a sick child.

She continued to play possum, all the while on the verge of hysteria. Jarred put his palm on her forehead, then ran his fingers back through her sweat-soaked hair. It was a gentle touch, but it terrified her.

His hand left her then and he seemed to reach for something. She heard the sound of water dripping into a container, then a cool cloth was against her cheek. Jarred washed her face and neck, then gingerly pressed the cloth against the side of her head, just above her temple. The pain there was intense and she realized that was where her head had struck the rock. After holding the compress there for several minutes, he put the cloth back into the container that was somewhere over her head, on a ledge, perhaps.

He was capable of kindness. Perhaps then, she could reason with him. And this was the time to find out.

Yet she couldn't find the courage to open her eyes and look at him, to speak to him, confront him if necessary. She felt so battered and weak, it was easier to do nothing, to bide her time and wait.

After another minute, he moved back and got to his feet, apparently satisfied with her condition. As he retreated, his robe dropped away and, lifting her head slightly, she had a glimpse of his magnificent physique.

Victoria's head fell back again as the cave returned to darkness. She was utterly exhausted. She needed medical attention, that was certain. She couldn't feign unconsciousness forever. The next time he came to her, she would try to speak to him. If she was to live, she'd need water and food. How long had she been here? It could have been days.

She sighed with despair. Maybe she should let herself die. It might be easier. Her condition might be hopeless anyway.

Tears began running down her cheeks and she tried hard not to cry aloud. She didn't want to bring him to her again.

In the vast silence she heard a faint moan, a distant sound. Was it him? No, it sounded like the wind. Could it be a storm? Had the snows come? If so, she could be stranded for months, if she lived that long.

Oh, God, she thought, please help me. And then she began to cry in earnest. This time, as she drifted into unconsciousness, it was for real.

5

JARRED SAT staring into the fire, thinking. For years now, life had been a seamless web. His days had been mostly the same, small things setting them apart, the occasional event making a given one truly memorable.

Having a woman in his cave was such a break with the usual challenges of survival that he wasn't sure how to deal with it. It had been years since he'd been around anyone in need. Never had he made the difference between life and death for someone. Initially his instinct to help had been strong, overriding his self-protectiveness. Now he feared he'd made a mistake in bringing her to his cave.

One thing was certain. His life would never be the same—even if the woman died. They would come searching for her, and that meant they'd be searching for him. And God only knew what had happened to Steve Parnell. The woman had given him a good clunk on the head before she'd run off. What was her name? Vicky. That's what Parnell had called her.

Jarred pulled on the ends of his beard. The whole business down at the camp had been weird. He still hadn't figured out why she and Parnell had been fighting. If she'd agreed to come camping alone with him, then they were probably lovers. But if so, why had Parnell tried to rape her?

And if they weren't lovers, then what was she doing with Parnell in the first place? Could she have come because of *him*? She had spoken his name just before Parnell had jumped her, and then again before she ran away. "Jarred, I'm your friend," she'd said. Had she uttered those words because she was a friend, or had she been conspiring with Parnell to trap him?

Jarred put another piece of wood on the fire and pulled the fur around his shoulders, shaking his head as he stared blankly at the flames. The cave felt different with a woman around, even an unconscious woman. No one had ever visited him there before, not even Macky Bean, though old Macky was usually drunk enough that he could have been here several times and not have known it. Jarred smiled at the thought of the grizzled old codger babbling at him in one of his drunken stupors.

But this Vicky wasn't Macky Bean. She was potentially real trouble. Yet in a way, having a woman in the cave was appealing. God knows, he'd fantasized often enough about having one with him.

Struggling up the mountain with her slung over his shoulder, he'd thought about how he'd wrapped her naked body in his coat, how he was actually carrying her off to his secret hiding place, where they'd be alone. It had been insane to take the risk, yet something made him do it—for himself as much as for her.

Since they had gotten back to the cave, he'd thought a lot about the way she'd looked lying by the fire naked, her skin so soft to the touch, so smooth, her curves so inviting, so womanly. It had been like seeing Tracey again, naked in the moonlight, remembering the feel of her flesh, the sensation of being inside her, holding her...except that this Vicky was unconscious, perhaps even dying.

Amazingly, he wanted her to live. She'd survived this long, and it would be unfair if she were to die now, before he'd found out what she was like, or why she'd called out to him. "Jarred, I'm your friend," she'd said. Had she uttered those words because she was afraid, or was there some other reason?

The fire was hot and Jarred stepped back a ways. He wiped the sweat off his forehead, and let the fur slip from his shoulders. Over the crackling of the blaze, he heard a sound from the sleeping cave. He cocked his ear. Was she crying or murmuring in her sleep? His heart pounding, he started to go to her, then he stopped himself.

Damn it, what was happening to him? He'd spent years trying to hate them all, every last one of them, and now this woman was making him act like a little boy. If it was people he wanted, he knew where to get them. He'd gone months—more than a year once—without speaking to another soul. Macky had been enough in the past. So why this obsession now?

Jarred had been so worried about her dying that he hadn't given a lot of thought to what he'd do if she lived. She'd probably want to leave as soon as she could, and that could be dangerous for him. The snows were coming and that would change things, too. The searchers might not come to the mountains in time. And then there would be no walking out . . . not easily.

What it meant, he realized, was that she might be there for months—assuming she lived. That would put a strain on his larder. He'd either have to kill another deer or risk a trip to see Macky. But how could he get away to do that? What would happen if she were too ill for him to leave? And if she was better, it could be risky leaving her alone. She might escape and lead his enemies to him.

Cursing the damnable situation, Jarred picked up a log and angrily threw it against the wall of the cave. Why hadn't he just left her to die? He wasn't used to these kinds of problems. There were plenty of damned good reasons why he'd left the world behind in the first place.

He drew in a calming breath, telling himself they hadn't beaten him to this point, and he wouldn't let them beat him now. This Vicky was in *his* home, even if it was just a cave. If she lived, she would have to do as *he* wished, whether she liked it or not. It would not be easy for either of them, but she would have to understand that she owed him. After all, he'd saved her life.

Jarred contemplated that for a moment. It was a weird thought. There was a woman in his cave, and she owed him her life.

VICTORIA AWOKE to the feeling of a cold, damp cloth on her battered head. Her eyes opened and she saw Jarred, his blue eyes peering directly into hers. His tangled hair and beard made him seem so large and wild that she was startled, her heart rising to her throat. When she gasped, he leaned back, but his expression didn't alter. There was wariness in his eyes, and suspicion.

She waited, holding her breath, expecting him to say something, but he didn't. He remained impassive for a long moment. If anything, his expression hardened. The look in his eye wasn't exactly crazed, and he didn't seem quite as ferocious as he had that night in the camp, but she could detect no hint of compassion in him. And yet he'd brought her here, nursed her.

Victoria swallowed hard. She tried to move her limbs but discovered she was too weak. Even breathing alone was a chore. She was completely helpless.

She searched his eyes for a clue to his attitude. What was he thinking? Couldn't he speak? Was he mentally unbalanced? They continued looking into each other's eyes until she managed to push a word out of her parched throat. "Jarred..."

He didn't respond. He was so impassive that he seemed almost cruel. Her eyes bubbled with tears.

"Can't you talk?" she murmured.

He continued his silent vigil, though he didn't really look much like the mute beast he seemed to be. She noticed then he had on a worn and tattered flannel shirt. He was dressed like a man, and that gave her hope. If only she wasn't so weak. She took a few breaths. "I must talk to you," she said.

"Why?"

She sighed, relieved that he at least sounded human. "Because nobody else has."

His eyes narrowed slightly. He looked skeptical. She tried to say something else, to explain, but her head was throbbing so hard it was difficult to keep her eyes focused. She let them close. Her breathing was shallow. She felt hot and feverish. After a minute she managed to open her eyes again. Jarred hadn't moved; his expression hadn't changed. He seemed to be waiting.

It suddenly occurred to her that he was on a death watch. She was about to die. This was a last farewell, and she was sharing it with the only living creature at hand.

She noticed that the light was much brighter than before. In the corner of her eye, she spotted a lantern. And there was daylight coming from the entrance to the chamber.

"How long have I been here?" she croaked.

He stared at her for a full minute before answering. "Two nights."

"Two?" He could have said anything. A week, a month, a century. She wouldn't have known the difference.

Damn his implacable face! There was no compassion in it, even as he watched her die.

She tried to swallow. It was difficult. Her throat was so dry. "I'm thirsty," she whispered. "Could I have some water?"

He rose to his knees, reaching for something above her head. She saw then that he was wearing a tattered pair of jeans, which, like the shirt, seemed incongruous.

He held a ceramic cup before her face. Slipping his hand behind her neck, he lifted her head so she could drink. It took all her energy to swallow, but the taste was divine. The longer he held the cup there, the more eagerly she drank. When she'd had enough, he set her head gently back onto the bed. Then he resumed his curious vigil, sitting back on his heels.

Her lids too heavy to keep open, Victoria closed her eyes. For the next several minutes, she drifted in and out of consciousness, wavering between dream and reality. Whenever she came to and opened her eyes, he was still there, watching over her.

She must have slept for a long while because she didn't wake again until she felt the cool cloth on her face. His expression remained grim, but there was a gentleness about him that was evident in the way he nursed her.

"You're being very kind to me," she said.

He worked his jaw, evidently contemplating what she'd said, though he didn't respond.

"Don't you like to talk?"

His only response was to put the cup of water to her lips again. Sighing, Victoria took the cup herself, though he did have to help her sit up. When the bearskin slid off her breast, she remembered her nakedness, and the fact that he'd undressed her. She watched him as he eased her back down onto the bed and covered her up again. He gave no indication of having noticed her nudity, though she knew he had.

When she was resting comfortably, her fingers clutching the fur to her throat, he finally spoke. "Why were you with Steve Parnell?"

Victoria understood then. He didn't trust her. That's why he was behaving this way. "So I could meet you, Jarred," she replied, struggling to sound both calm and logical. "Parnell told me he could find you."

For the first time, Jarred's expression changed. He smiled bitterly. "Parnell is always trying to find me. And always with a rifle. He wanted to kill me, and so did you!"

"No," she protested. "That's not true!"

"I don't believe you," he shouted back angrily.

His wrath frightened her and Victoria's heart began beating wildly with fear. She tried to steady herself, realizing she couldn't afford to anger him. "That wasn't the reason I came, Jarred. I stopped Parnell from shooting you, remember? I didn't want him to hurt you."

He grunted, but didn't speak.

She couldn't let his silences get to her. "You see, I think your life is very interesting and I wanted to know about it. I wanted to help you."

He tugged on the ends of his beard, regarding her with suspicion. When he finally spoke, his voice was low and very measured. And he sounded quite sure of himself. "I don't want any help. Not from you. Not from anybody."

This wasn't the time to get into her reasons for being there, Victoria realized. Nor was it the right time to be persuasive. Besides, she was too weak for a prolonged discussion. She studied him as he studied her. He was deeply suspicious of her, that was evident, and curious, too. She might be able to use that to her advantage.

"Why did you save my life, Jarred?"

He thought for a moment. "Because I'm a fool."

"You're not a fool," she said. "You're a decent person, and I'm grateful."

His eyes narrowed. "I'm not a child, Vicky. Don't talk to me like that."

Her brows rose. "Why did you call me Vicky?"

"Parnell called you that. Isn't it your name?"

"No," she said. "It's Victoria. Parnell is a chauvinistic bastard who refused to call me by my proper name."

Jarred smiled. She realized then how incongruous her anger must have sounded. It also occurred to her that she didn't know what had happened to Parnell, how severely she'd injured him. "Is he all right?"

He shrugged. "I don't know. He could be dead. I hope so."

The words stabbed at her.

"You mean I killed him?"

"Maybe."

"Oh, Lord," she moaned. "I didn't mean to hurt him. Not badly."

"Either way, they will come."

"Who?"

"The sheriff. If Parnell was able to walk out, he will tell them what happened. If he didn't make it back to town, they will come looking for him. And unless the winter comes first, they will find his body."

Victoria shivered at the matter-of-factness of his words, the horror they implied. She might have killed a man! Her eyes filled with tears. She glanced at Jarred. There was accusation in his eyes. "You blame me, don't you?"

He just stared at her, his mouth drawn into a hard line.

"Don't be bitter, Jarred. You don't understand. People don't hate you. Parnell is not typical. I—"

He suddenly got to his feet, startling her. As he glared down at her, she saw the beast again. The man she'd been trying to talk to had vanished. There was pure hatred in the eyes of the creature standing over her.

"This is my place!" he roared. "Don't tell me what to do here, or what to think. *I* decide. Don't tell me anything, Victoria . . . whoever you are." With that, he turned and stomped out of the chamber.

She was so shocked by the outburst that she began to cry. All the emotion that had been pent-up in her came boiling out. She was sick and miserable and helpless and not far from death. Her sobs turned mournful.

After a few minutes Jarred reappeared. He stood at the entrance of the small cave and regarded her sullenly. The light from the lantern was not strong but, through her tears, she thought she detected ambivalence on his face.

"Are you hungry?" he asked. "Do you want food?"

Victoria had been so caught up in her predicament that she hadn't been aware of how hungry she was. "Yes, I would like something. I feel very weak."

He turned and left the chamber. A moment later he returned with a flannel shirt. When he got close enough, he held it out to her.

She took the shirt and clutched it to her breast. "Where are my clothes?"

"At the creek. They were wet and soaked with blood, so I took them off you."

Victoria colored, thinking of him undressing her as she lay unconscious. How long had it been since he'd seen a woman's body? What had been going through his mind?

"I will help you," he announced.

She wanted to say she would dress herself, but being unable even to lift her head, she knew she couldn't. It was easiest to submit—Jarred could do with her as he wished anyway, so there was no point in arguing.

He pulled back the bearskin. She recoiled instinctively, feebly drawing up her knees and covering her breasts with her arms. Jarred ignored her, pulling her up to a sitting position, and helping her into the shirt. Then he eased her back down and buttoned the shirt as she lay trembling.

She watched his eyes, wondering if there was lust in his heart. Observing him closely, she did note a sign of awareness—the tiniest flicker in his eyes, the subtle flair of his nostrils as he drew in a breath. She judged he was keeping his feelings to himself more out of pride than consideration.

Next thing she knew, Jarred was wrapping her in a large piece of deerskin to which rabbit fur had been sewn, the soft side against her skin. He silently slid his arms under her legs and back and stood upright, lifting her effortlessly. It was only then that Victoria fully appreciated his size and strength.

She took a deep breath, wondering where he was taking her. As he held her against him, she looked around. They were in a small chamber that was used as a kind of bedroom. Jarred carried her through a low passageway to the main room, where the ceiling was much higher. A fire was burning in a pit in the center of the room. Smoke drifted into the craggy ceiling and disappeared. Incredibly, the room was furnished with rough-hewn, makeshift furniture, including a wooden table and a rocking chair, probably pillaged from a remote cabin.

Various cooking utensils, tools, lanterns were lying about on surfaces or hanging on the walls. A rifle was leaning next to a crude sideboard. The most surprising sight of all was a large window that admitted sufficient light to illuminate the chamber. Jarred carried her directly to it so she could see out.

After the darkness of the bedchamber, the light seemed very bright. With a shock, Victoria realized the glaring white was snow. When Jarred wiped the glass with his elbow, she was able to see snowflakes swirling outside, and she felt the cold radiating through the makeshift barrier.

"It's snowing," she said, the alarm in her voice evident.

"The more it snows, the harder it is for them to come after us," he replied.

She gave him a questioning look. He didn't let her wonder about the implications for long.

"You won't be leaving soon," he said.

She was trapped. He didn't elaborate, but he might as well have added, "Which means you are my prisoner."

She had no intention of leaving it at that, but sensed it wasn't the time to discuss what would happen in the coming days. First she needed to get back her health and recover her strength.

Victoria thought if she could get him to express himself, she'd could at least figure out what was on his mind. She needed a topic for conversation. The window! She never would have expected that kind of luxury. . . not in a cave. "Where did you get the window?" she asked.

"I have my ways," he replied tersely.

The window was built into a wall fashioned from poles that had been lashed together, the cracks sealed with mud. The narrow door next to it was covered with a multilayered leather flap that was tied down securely and weighted at the bottom with a large rock.

Jarred abruptly turned from the window and carried her to the rocking chair, which he dragged close to the fire with his foot. Then he set her in it, standing back to consider the sight of her. He seemed pleased with himself. It was a distinct improvement from the dour expression on his face when she first awoke.

"What are you thinking, Jarred?" she asked, finally deciding to meet the situation head-on. "What are you planning to do with me?"

He gazed at her, showing no particular desire to respond. She stared back, beginning to understand that he wasn't going to allow her to manipulate him. He would be doing things his way, not hers. The point wasn't lost on him that she was weak, sick and vulnerable. She could only hope that the humanity she'd seen in him thus far was not an illusion.

"I didn't come here willingly," she prodded. "You brought me here."

"Maybe I should have left you in the creek." He turned then and went across the room, where he rummaged through some large handwoven baskets made of sticks, and returned with an apple and a knife. He began slicing the fruit.

"Jarred, I'm sorry if I sounded ungrateful."

His response was to hand her a piece of fruit.

"Why did you bring me here?"

"Maybe because you're a woman."

Was the truth finally coming out? Had Parnell been right all along? "What do you mean by that?" she asked, trying to keep the tremor out of her voice.

"If it had been Steve Parnell in the creek, I would have left him to drown."

Jarred was toying with her. Arguing was useless. What she really needed was time . . . time to think, to gain his confidence, to grow stronger. She bit into the piece of apple, munching ravenously. He gave her another slice, which she ate with equal enthusiasm.

"Where did you get the apples?" she asked, remembering that she had at first awakened to the smell.

"I have my ways," he said, handing her another piece.

"Why won't you tell me?" she pressed. "Don't you trust me? Is that it?"

He didn't answer.

"Jarred?"

He handed her the rest of the apple. "Just eat, Victoria." He went to the window again, his back to her, and looked out at the falling snow.

She watched him as she munched on the apple, her body soaking up the nourishment practically as fast as she could swallow. It had been days since she'd eaten. No wonder she was weak.

When she'd finished, she leaned back against the rocker. Her temples were pounding. She couldn't ever remember having such a blinding headache.

Ignoring the pain, her eyes drifted over to him. She noticed again how broad-shouldered and strong Jarred was. Were it not for the crown of shaggy hair and the handmade moccasins, he might have been a bulldogger in the rodeo. He had the size and strength for wrestling steers.

He turned around then and peered at her across the cave. "Do you want more food?"

"I could eat, but I'm awfully tired. Maybe I should lie down for a while."

He silently left the window and headed for the sleeping room in the cave. He returned a moment later with the bearskin. He spread it out on the floor next to the fire. Then he lifted her from the chair, looking into her eyes with an aloofness bordering on disdain as he put her down on the pallet he'd made.

After making sure she was comfortable, he went to where he'd gotten the apple and returned with a small bowl of nuts and venison jerky, which he placed on the floor beside her. Then he tossed another piece of wood onto the fire and went back to the window. It seemed to be his favorite place.

Victoria watched him as she nibbled on the nuts. She was feeling stronger by the minute, and now that death wasn't so imminent, she was able to take stock of the situation. Jarred wasn't the wild man she'd expected. He had a subtlety and complexity that was surprising.

Her presence clearly troubled him, though. It had to be difficult for him to deal with another human being after being alone so long. And yet, that fascinated her, as well. Everything about him and the situation was remarkable. Still, she hadn't a hope in hell of engaging him in meaningful conversation about it until she'd won his trust.

"Do you want me to tell you about myself?" she asked. "Do you want to know why I came to Edgar to find you?"

He turned around slowly and stared at her, waiting.

"I'm an instructor at the University of California," she said. "And also a graduate student. I heard about you from one of my professors, and I had to come. I had to know what your life is like."

"Is that the truth?"

"Yes. Honestly."

"And you didn't know Steve Parnell before?"

"No. Like I told you, I met him just before he brought me to the mountains. Associating myself with him was a terrible mistake. I know I've created some problems for you, but I hope you'll give me the benefit of the doubt."

Jarred lapsed into another of his silences. It was disconcerting to watch him staring at her, brooding and uncommunicative. One minute he seemed practically normal and the next he withdrew, leaving her uncertain about him and confused.

He went to the back of the cave to fetch the handmade buckskin coat he'd worn that night at the camp. He slipped it on as he returned to the front of the cave, scarcely paying any attention to her as he walked by.

"Where are you going?" she asked as he lifted the flap covering the door.

He glanced back. "I must see how deep the snow is on the mountain. I need to know if they will be coming."

6

VICTORIA WASN'T quite sure when she had fallen asleep. When she awoke she found a large ceramic bowl next to her, full of apples and jerky, nuts and berries. There was also a can of water and some extra wood. The only light came from the fire, and it was barely flickering. She glanced toward the window and saw that it was dark.

"Jarred?" she called. There was no response. The only sound was the crackling of the fire. She tried again. "Jarred?" Still no answer.

Victoria assumed he'd left again, but why at night? She noticed that his rifle was gone. That sent a tremor through her. Had he spotted a search party? Or perhaps a campfire in the valley?

Victoria's pulse picked up at the thought. Her head still ached and, though she felt better than she had earlier, the pain made it difficult to reason things through. It didn't make sense that Jarred would go after a search party—that would be asking for trouble. On the other hand, if he *was* out stalking, that could mean that help was near. Her intellectual curiosity might have brought her to the mountain in the first place, but so far nothing had turned out the way she'd planned. She needed medical attention. And there was no telling how things would develop with Jarred if she was stuck in the cave for weeks on end. He might treat her all right. How could she count on it when he was so volatile—gentle one moment, cold and inscrutable the next.

Between the earlier meal and the sleep, she'd regained perhaps half her strength. Despite her headache she was fairly comfortable curled up in the fur-lined deerskin blanket.

The wind began howling, rattling the window. Then a chilling thought came to her. What if he had already encountered a search party? If he'd been killed or seriously hurt, they would have no way of finding her.

She was upsetting herself unnecessarily. Jarred had made it on his own this long, she could see no reason why he would falter now, unless her presence had so distressed him, he'd lost his judgment.

Her initial impression of Jarred had been way off track. Despite the frustrating silences, he could talk well enough when he wanted to. He didn't seem like a man who hadn't spoken to another human being in fifteen years.

As wary and uneasy as Jarred could be at times, he was surprisingly serene, in tune with his surroundings. And unlike most people she knew, he seemed content. It was intriguing to think how mentally, emotionally and spiritually strong he must be.

Something about the man compelled her. Jarred had a strength of character that was most impressive. To say he was manly was an understatement. Even with a shaggy beard and unkempt hair, he was physically attractive. When she thought about it, that was the most surprising aspect of all. At the campsite, when she had

had her first glimpse of him, he had seemed like a raging beast. Now she'd learned that wasn't true.

Hungry again, Victoria ate some fruit and nuts, knowing she had to build her strength. Then she slept.

The next time she awoke it was daylight. Between the rest and the food, she felt much better. The storm had abated. There was no sign of Jarred. That concerned her. Deciding to explore the cave, she wrapped the deerskin around her like a robe, stood up and took a few unsteady steps across the cold floor.

After perusing the various utensils Jarred had made or scrounged, she picked up his moccasins. They were crudely made, lined with rabbit fur for warmth. The man was clearly inventive. How few people there were anymore who could be thoroughly self-sufficient.

Victoria slipped the moccasins on. They were so large that she felt like a child wearing her father's shoes. Jarred was tall, probably around six-four. Yet, his imposing physical presence no longer bothered her.

Having discovered he wasn't a raving maniac, Victoria assumed that once she had his trust, they would be able to talk. There were a million things about his experience that she wanted to discuss with him. Did he wonder what was going on in the world? Who was president? Or what basketball teams were winning?

His reflections on life and man's place in the universe had to be different from most people's. The importance of society, the meaning of family and relationships—it would be interesting to discover how fifteen years alone had colored his views on all those issues.

What an incredible story. And how fortunate she was to stumble onto it. Of course, there would be a price. To Jarred, her arrival was not another interesting little diversion, an intellectual adventure. He'd said she was a problem to him, and Victoria knew it was true.

Admittedly, she had brushed that aspect of it aside too easily. She guiltily acknowledged she'd been blindly insensitive to the effect of her interference in Jarred's life, treating him as if he were a specimen she could slide under a microscope. And given the way things were working out, she couldn't help feeling ashamed of the arrogance of her presumptions and behavior.

Her shame over that made her start to worry again. Where was Jarred? Had she driven him away? Impelled him into danger? Victoria went to the window and wiped it so that she could see out. The snow had drifted to the bottom of the pane. A few flakes continued to swirl, but mostly the sky was clear. She could see the snowy peaks across the valley. Winter seemed to stretch to infinity. That was probably the way Jarred viewed the world—a place that changed only with the will of nature.

As she stood at the window, she thought she heard a faint sound. The fire crackled occasionally, but this sound was more remote—the hum and throb of an engine. When it grew louder, she realized it was a helicopter.

Moments later, she saw the chopper cruising above the ridge line across the valley. Her heart quickened. It was flying in a deliberate pattern, in all likelihood searching for her. Had they found Steve Parnell's Jeep? Were they now looking for the two of them? Or had

Parnell managed to walk out and were they searching for her and Jarred?

As Victoria watched, the aircraft moved on up the valley and disappeared. Had she just lost a golden opportunity for escape? Jarred may have saved her life, but could she rely on him to get her back to civilization?

A few minutes later the sound of the chopper's engine grew louder again. Victoria looked out the window. She couldn't spot it, but from the sound she figured it was probably coming back up the valley, perhaps along the ridge on her side. If so, all she had to do was push her way through the snow outside the cave and get out onto the ledge. She could wave a cloth and attract the attention of the pilot. They could either lift her out, or direct a ground party to the location.

Victoria knew she had to act fast. She was no longer in danger of dying from her injuries. Nonetheless, God only knew how long she might be trapped in this cave. What if Jarred didn't return? Could she survive alone? And if he was okay, did she have the right to betray the location of his cave to the outside world, just so she could make a quick and easy trip back to civilization?

Ambivalent thoughts were swirling through her head as the throb of the engine grew louder and louder. Victoria glanced back into the cave, trying to decide what was right. Judging by the sound, the helicopter was nearly overhead, and if she was going to attract the attention of the helicopter pilot, she had to do so at once. She leaned close to the glass, looking up at the sky, her mind and heart tugging in opposite directions.

And then the aircraft passed overhead, its shadow flashing across the snowbank outside the cave. She stood motionless, her heart pounding, aware that the opportunity had been lost. Tears welled in her eyes and she dropped her head. She might have made a fatal mistake.

Slowly she became aware of the cold radiating through the window. She shivered. Why had she lost her nerve? It wasn't so that she could continue her research. Her academic interest had become secondary. Jarred Wilde now mattered to her as a human being.

Wiping her eyes, Victoria wondered why that should come as such a revelation. He *was* human, after all. Was she feeling some other attachment to him she didn't understand? Maybe she'd empathized too much and was making the mistake of the physician who let herself get too emotionally involved with her patient. Or maybe she'd simply let her injury cloud her judgment.

Clutching her blanket tightly about her, Victoria turned from the window. For a few minutes she warmed herself by the fire, brooding. Finally she got up, hoping to distract herself by continuing her exploration of his cave.

She wandered through a third chamber at the rear of the main cave. In it she found an impressive stock of supplies—cords of wood, a barrel of water, animal skins, ammunition, boxes of matches, even oil for the lantern. There were more apples, a few potatoes and carrots, and several dozen cans of food.

She went back to the sleeping chamber where she'd first awakened. Little natural light reached that corner of the cave so she lit the lantern. Jarred had made a second sleeping place for himself, having given her the principal spot. In the corner he had a stash of personal items.

There was a ten-year-old almanac, a handbook of flora and fauna of the Pacific Northwest, and a desk copy of a medical encyclopedia—all appearing well read—and a wooden crate containing an amazing assortment of books. Curious, Victoria picked through them. On top were essays by Thoreau and Emerson, as well as Viktor Frankl's book, *Man's Search for Meaning*. There were tomes of philosophy, including Rousseau, Hobbes, Voltaire and John Stuart Mill. She was amazed.

In addition to the more serious books, there were volumes of poetry and works of fiction, as well as a number of science fiction paperbacks. Some of the books contained the stamp of the Lewis County Library. How could Jarred have gotten library books? Other volumes, especially the fiction, had the name "Macky Bean" written in pencil on the inside cover. Could Jarred have stolen the books from someone's cabin?

Turning from the books, she found a small basket of mementos from Jarred's past. Among them a belt buckle, a key ring, a few coins, a paper clip, a ballpoint pen and a badly worn wallet. Victoria knew she was snooping, but she wanted to learn as much as she could about Jarred Wilde.

Opening a leather wallet, she discovered his "official" life suspended at the age of eighteen. Under yellowing plastic there was a driver's license with a photo of a handsome young man with thick black hair falling across his forehead, a thin yet masculine face and a smile that was tragically ironic, considering his fate.

The wallet contained several other photographs. One was of an attractive young woman with long black hair. She was wearing a miniskirt and holding the hand of a little boy. Victoria assumed it was Jarred with his mother. She studied it closely, as Jarred must have a thousand times.

The next photograph was of a soldier, a tall young man in camouflage fatigues and jungle boots. The shape of the face and the general build were much like Jarred's. Victoria assumed the man was his father. There was also a school picture of a pretty blond teenager, presumably Tracey Emerson, the girl he'd fought over with Todd Parnell.

The last was a snapshot of the same girl. This one was a full-length picture of her in a bikini, posing coquettishly. On the back in an immature hand was written, "For you, Jarred, so you'll always remember!"

There were a few other items—four years of student cards, a fifteen-year-old wallet calendar, a fishing license and a five dollar bill that seemed as ancient as Lincoln himself. That was it. Jarred's past.

Victoria put the wallet back in the basket, her eyes teary with emotion. How tragic it seemed that these few photographs should be his sole connection with the outside world, with his past. His parents were gone, so he could never have more than pictures and mementos. How did Jarred deal with the loss of Tracey Emerson? How could he cut himself off so completely from everything they'd shared?

Victoria had had several high school boyfriends, though no one so important as Tracey seemed to have been to Jarred. If there had been someone, she couldn't imagine denying herself, as he had done. What remarkable strength and will. Yet how sad.

Victoria went back to the main cave. The wind had come up again, its moan sounding particularly melancholy. If the helicopter were to return now, she wouldn't even be tempted to flag it down, though maybe at some point in the future she would, if it became clear that Jarred would try to keep her from leaving.

She'd done the right thing. Regardless of what happened to her, it would have been tragic to destroy the life that Jarred had made for himself. Besides, if it wasn't for him, she already would have died, so in a sense she owed him that much anyway.

After a while she ate again. Then, as the day wore on, she grew progressively more worried. By far, the worst part was the unrelenting loneliness. How had Jarred endured this for fifteen long years?

Exhausted, she napped. Then, just as daylight was waning, she heard a thumping sound at the entrance to the cave. She stared at the door. Was it Jarred, or might it be a rescue party?

The heavy leather door opened and Jarred pushed his way through the wall of snow. He was bundled in leather and fur. A rifle in hand. He resembled a nineteenth-century frontiersman, his beard white with frost, vapor billowing from his mouth. He glanced at her before putting the rifle down and turning back outside. He returned a moment later dragging a large buck by the antlers. Once the carcass had cleared the entrance, he let the head drop with a thud.

Jarred made a halfhearted attempt to secure the door, then stepped over the buck and staggered toward the fire, dropping to his knees. He pulled off his leather mittens and tossed them aside. His eyebrows and lashes were covered with frost. Steam rose from his body, and within moments his face began glistening as the frost and ice turned to water.

He was panting, each tortured breath ending in a wheeze. He held his hands close to the fire, rubbing them briskly to get the circulation going. Then he began removing his outer garments. Midway through the process, he stopped. His shoulders slumped and he looked over at her again.

"Are you all right?" she asked.

He nodded, showing no sign of wishing to communicate. Victoria waited a few minutes, trying to assess his mood, his state of mind.

"I was worried about you," she said. "I was afraid something might have happened, that you'd been hurt or captured."

He gave a fierce look. "They tried."

"You mean the helicopter?"

"Yes. Did you hear it?"

"I was at the window when I saw it fly over. I figured they were looking for us."

"Why didn't you flag them down? They would have seen you if you'd gone onto the ledge. I thought you might try."

"I considered it," she admitted. "But I knew if I did, you'd be compromised. I thought I owed it to you, not to betray you."

Jarred listened, reflecting on her words as he gazed at the fire. Victoria waited for some kind of response, but got none.

"Why did you go out in the storm?" she asked.

"We need extra food."

"You mean, you went out in this weather because of me?"

"The more it snows, the harder it is to hunt. I couldn't wait any longer." He struggled to get his coat off, then threw it aside. He wiped his damp face with his shirt sleeve. Between the melted snow and sweat, he was soaked.

"There's a solution, Jarred," she said. "If I leave, you won't have to worry about having enough food for the winter."

"It's too late for that, Victoria."

"What do you mean?"

"The snow is already too deep to travel, and another storm is coming. I almost didn't make it back. The last mile I had to drag the buck. I was too weak to carry him anymore."

Victoria looked over at the dead animal, then at Jarred. "Well, I can't stay here, so I've got to go. There's no other choice."

"If you try to walk out of the mountains, you'll die. You're too weak. And by the time you regain your strength, the snow will make it impossible."

Her expression turned accusing. "I don't believe you."

He didn't reply.

"I don't think you're telling the truth," she insisted. "I think you *want* me to stay here."

He sat impassively, not moving a muscle.

"I'm not your prisoner, Jarred. You have no right to keep me here."

Struggling to his feet, he went to the larder and gathered some food, pausing to stuff a bite or two into his mouth. He drank some water, then sat in front of the fire, ignoring her completely.

Victoria was fuming. Only hours before, she'd regretted interfering in his life—and now he was interfering in hers! But she knew there was no point in aggravating him—at least not until she found out exactly what it was he wanted.

After he'd eaten, Jarred sprawled out on his back, appearing utterly exhausted. Victoria guiltily got to her feet and filled a drinking can with water, bringing it to him.

Jarred glanced up at the offering with surprise, taking it without comment. He drank the water, then lay back again.

When he didn't respond, Victoria decided silence was a game two could play as easily as one. Ten or fifteen minutes passed before Jarred spoke. "I went by the camp. Parnell's body was not there. The snow covered the tracks so I don't know if he was taken away or if he walked out. They know about him for sure. We don't have until spring."

"Will they find the cave?"

"Not unless we want them to. Now they can only come by air."

"Once I'm gone, you'll be safe," she said, hoping the logic would appeal to him.

"Maybe."

"If I wanted to betray you, I could have gone out when the helicopter came by. But I didn't. So I think you should trust me."

"I trust no one but myself."

"Well, damn it, maybe it's something you should learn to do."

He turned his eyes on her, but not accusingly. He seemed more uncertain about how to deal with her change in mood than anything else. "I thought of you while I was gone," he said matter-of-factly. "Last night I slept under a log with the body of the deer over me to protect me against the storm. It was very cold and I thought I might die. I pictured you sleeping by the fire wrapped in the rabbit fur. I knew I had to bring back the buck."

The sentiment touched her—it was the closest he'd come to friendliness. Still, she didn't much care for the way he'd brushed aside the prospect of her leaving.

Victoria suddenly realized she was nervous in his presence. Jarred was so unpredictable. The last time they'd talked, she hadn't been far from death. Now they were on a more equal plane.

And for the first time, she sensed a strong sexual energy that was focused squarely on her. The way his gaze kept gravitating toward her, it was evident that he was as aware of it as she. Victoria pulled the blanket tightly around her.

"How do you feel?" he asked. "Does your head ache?"

"Yes, but I am much stronger. I guess I just needed some food and more rest."

"I'm tired myself," he said, wearily. "I have to get out of these wet clothes." He removed the skins tied around his feet, revealing an old pair of boots, which he took off. Then he got up.

He began removing his shirt. She wasn't sure how far he intended to go. He wouldn't strip in front of her, would he?

Under his flannel shirt was a tattered undershirt, which he removed, his shoulders and arms glistening in the firelight. She stared at the dense mat of hair on his muscular chest. Stripped to the waist, he removed his outer pants, leaving only the worn pair of jeans.

Jarred stood bare-chested in the firelight. He was not exactly preening, but neither was he hiding his rugged masculinity. He was simply a physical creature and she was responding strongly to his animal magnetism.

Jarred stiffly walked to the far corner of the cave. She watched as he stripped completely naked and began washing himself from a large pan of water.

He was ignoring her, and Victoria tried not to look at him. But from time to time her eye was drawn to his magnificent physique. It was hard to tell how conscious he was of his effect on her. The question was whether he was thinking of her, the same way she was thinking of him.

His sexuality had been in the background from the start. Even before she and Steve Parnell had come to the high country, sex had been a major issue. Now she was in Jarred's cave with him and he was totally nude. The only thing left uncertain were his intentions.

Victoria lay on her pallet, her heart pounding with a quiet fear. She prayed he wouldn't attempt anything. But how reasonable an expectation was that? Jarred had done nothing to indicate a desire for her, though she had little knowledge of his attitudes toward anything.

He wrapped a deerskin blanket around himself, then he sat down cross-legged, the blanket completely hiding his body as he resumed his contemplation of the fire.

Victoria lay with her head resting on her arm, watching the flames. Long minutes passed in silence. He absolutely refused to give any indication of his state of mind.

"I looked around the cave while you were gone," she said, hoping to start him talking. "You have quite a variety of things. Not quite all the comforts of home," she said with a smile, "but almost."

Jarred nodded, his expression cautious.

"Where did you get all your stuff? Did you scavenge it, or steal it, or what?"

"It isn't important."

"Parnell said he thought somebody was supplying you with things."

"He doesn't know anything."

"Is he wrong?"

"I said it isn't important," he repeated emphatically.

Victoria didn't like his truculence. "I wish you weren't so distrustful," she said. "I'm only trying to make polite conversation. People do that, you know."

"This is not a party," he said dryly.

"You've got that right."

He gave her a look.

"Who's Macky Bean?" she asked, determined to goad him into talking.

Jarred's eyes flashed. It was the most emotion he'd shown since he'd returned to the cave. "How do you know about Macky?"

Victoria saw instantly that her impetuousness had gotten her into trouble. There was no point in lying, so she pressed ahead bravely. "I happened to see your books."

"What do you mean, you *happened* to see my books?" he shouted. "You were snooping!"

"I didn't mean any harm," she said, taken aback by his fury. "I was curious."

He pointed an accusing finger, his face flushed. "Don't get curious with my things! Do you understand?"

His anger was so unexpected that she was speechless. She struggled to find words of apology, as tears welled up in her eyes. Rather than let him see her cry she rolled over, turning her back to the fire and to him. She bit her lip and tears spurted from her eyes—out of anger and hurt. She wiped them away, refusing to make a sound.

Minutes passed and nothing happened. Finally she turned and looked back at him. Jarred might as well have been a statute, he was so still. Exasperated, she lay her head on the bearskin.

Another minute passed, then Jarred said, "Did you look at my pictures?"

She couldn't lie to him. "Yes."

She expected fury. Instead there was only more unbearable silence. She refused to look at him again, though at this point it seemed this game could go on all night.

After a while he said, "I'm very tired. I have to get some sleep. Stay here. I'm going to the other room."

She heard him get to his feet, then pad off. He stopped at the entrance to the bedchamber.

"I'm sorry I yelled at you, Victoria," he said. Then he ducked into the dark side room, leaving her alone by the crackling fire.

7

AFTER JARRED HAD GONE off to bed, Victoria was too agitated to sleep. She went over and over her situation. For a while, especially after she'd gone through his personal effects, she was convinced she'd made the right decision when she hadn't tried to signal the helicopter. Now she wasn't so sure.

Things were not going well. It was nearly impossible to engage him in conversation. In time it might happen, but time was not her ally. They were being hunted, the snows were closing them in—even survival couldn't be taken for granted. And Jarred himself was volatile—confounding and unpredictable.

It was a relief that he hadn't turned out to be the sex-crazed monster Parnell had predicted. She was fortunate that there was an inherent decency in the man. He had saved her life and nursed her back to health. She wanted to like him, but Jarred refused to make it easy.

Staring into the shadows of the cave, she tried to understand him. He was a paradox—civilized and gentle, savage and intractable. He was man. He was beast.

In a perverse sort of way, she identified with Jarred Wilde. From the day Dr. Walther first told the story of the wild man of Edgar, she had felt a certain compassion for him. Now that she was in his cave, his battle was becoming hers. She was beginning to share his pathos and his struggle.

Victoria peered into the dark recesses of the cave, toward the spot where Jarred had bathed. His nudity had unnerved and embarrassed her. There was nothing monstrous about Jarred. To the contrary, he was a beautiful specimen. Adonis banished to the Underworld.

And he was evoking feelings in her that she was not fully prepared for. How did a woman come to terms with a man who was at once fantastical and endearing, alarming and alluring? He was no ordinary man.

The circumstances were too precarious to continue indefinitely. Jarred seemed to think that she would be there for the winter. How could she live with the man for three or four months as though she were only a weekend houseguest? Something would surely happen between them, and Victoria didn't think she could handle that.

When she finally fell asleep, she dreamed she was fleeing through the snow with someone in hot pursuit. Ironically her tormentor wasn't Jarred. It was Steve Parnell and a posse of townspeople.

By the time she awoke, Jarred had dressed the buck and was cleaning up. Victoria had seen a lot of gore around the ranch, so it did not upset her. She had always lived close to nature, watching calves and foals being born and seeing sick or ailing animals being put down. She'd watched a cougar taking a newborn calf in a snowy pasture and she'd seen a bear maul her dog. She knew about survival, yet she hadn't viscerally experienced what it was like to live so close to the edge as Jarred did.

She went over to where he was kneeling, scraping the hide of the buck with his knife. He was wearing a tattered undershirt and jeans. She was in the flannel shirt he'd given her.

He glanced at her bare legs, his eyes lingering for a moment before he looked up at her.

"Good morning," she said, ignoring the way he'd been looking at her.

"Good morning."

"I feel much better today."

"That's good."

"How about you?" she asked, determined to get a conversation going. "Did you sleep well?"

"Yes, I was tired."

He was at least answering her questions. That was progress. "Listen, I'm sorry I upset you. I shouldn't have looked at your things while you were gone. It was inconsiderate."

"Forget it," he said.

"I did it because I want to understand you. I had good intentions, I just made a poor choice."

He sat back on his haunches and stared up at her. With the light coming in the window she was able to see the deep blue of his eyes. She could almost imagine his face without the beard. The boy in the driver's license picture become a man was really extremely handsome.

When the slightest smile touched his lips, Victoria realized he was conscious of her study of him. She swallowed hard, struggling to maintain her composure. The last thing she needed was to give the impression she was sending signals.

"I'm not used to having someone around," he said, sounding as though he was making an apology himself. "Especially a woman."

"You've evidently adjusted to being alone."

"It's normal for me."

"I know. I must be a great burden to you."

"It's different. Even talking to someone feels peculiar. But I'm beginning to get used to it again."

"I'd like very much to understand your feelings," she said. "I'd like to hear about your experiences, your life."

"We'll have all winter to talk, Victoria. Before it's over, you'll be tired of my stories."

As he spoke, he was looking at her legs again. A shiver went through her. She knew right then that she couldn't possibly run around half-dressed all the time. That would be asking for trouble.

"Do you have anything else around here that I could wear?" she asked.

She noticed a slight smile on his face and wondered if he'd read her mind. If so, then he'd probably been thinking about her running around without proper clothes on, too.

"If you're cold, I'll put another log on the fire."

His tone had been neutral, but he was a lot more subtle than she'd given him credit for.

"Being cold isn't the issue, Jarred. I can't run around like this. Don't you have some pants or something? Maybe some deerskin I could wrap around like a skirt, anything."

He gave an impatient sigh and got to his feet. His hands were covered with blood. He wiped them on his pant legs and strode toward the storeroom. Victoria followed him.

"There are some clothes I found that were too small for me to wear," he said. He rummaged around through piles of can goods and other provisions until he located a pair of jeans. They were in excellent condition. "I found these in a cabin," he said, handing them to her.

She held them up. "I think they'll work if I roll up the cuffs and cinch in the waist."

"They're all yours," he said. "Put them on."

"Turn around first."

He did, but not with alacrity. Victoria rolled the cuffs a few turns and stepped into the jeans. Even after tucking in the shirt, there were a few extra inches at the waist.

"I don't suppose you have a belt around here."

Jarred turned, surveying her carefully. He didn't comment, but something told her he preferred her legs bare. He went to the corner where there was a pile of scrap leather and picked out a couple of rawhide thongs. She took the smaller one and threaded it through the belt loops.

"Do you have an old pair of boots that would fit me?" she asked hopefully.

"No," Jarred said, "but I was thinking I should make you some shoes."

"Today?"

"No, not today."

She was beginning to think he would do whatever he had to, to keep her from leaving. He certainly wouldn't make it easy for her to get out of there. She would have to pick her opportunities carefully, and yet she couldn't wait forever. Winter was definitely upon them. Even so, instinctively she knew he was exaggerating the difficulty of getting out of the mountains because it served his purposes—whatever they were.

Jarred left the storeroom and went back to the carcass. Victoria followed him, watching as he finished dressing the buck. She had just squatted down beside him when they heard the sound of an aircraft engine in the distance. They both got up and went to the window.

"They are searching for us again," he said.

Together they watched the aircraft fly along the far ridge, just as it had the day before. Victoria felt anxious. Jarred didn't look pleased, but he was calm.

"That helicopter would be a quick way for me to get out of here, wouldn't it?"

"Yes."

"Isn't there a way I could do it without giving away the location of the cave?"

"Not without getting far away from here first. And there isn't enough time for that."

"Couldn't I just go up on top of the ridge? I could say I was wandering along. I promise I wouldn't tell them where I'd been."

"No, it's too risky."

"You mean it's too risky for you, don't you?"

"I'm the one who has a lot to lose," he said, his voice hard.

"And what about me?" she asked, knowing her voice was shrill. "Do you think I want to spend the winter here? What if I got seriously ill?"

"You chose to come to the mountains, Victoria."

They were circling back into the same argument again. The difference this time was she had an opportunity to be rescued, and it was about to pass her by. She could hear the chopper approaching. It was on their side of the valley now. Jarred regarded her suspiciously.

"You don't want me to go," she charged. "You want to keep me a prisoner."

"I know them," he said. "They don't care about me."

The whirl of the aircraft grew louder. Victoria figured it would pass overhead in less than thirty seconds. If another storm was coming, this might be her last chance. For a moment she agonized. Jarred looked at her strangely, as if he knew what she was thinking. His eyes hardened.

Suddenly the realization hit her that he wanted a companion for the winter. A woman. It was as simple as that. He might not be the sex-crazed bastard that Steve Parnell was, neither was he St. Francis of Assisi.

"I'm going out there," she said firmly.

He shook his head. "No, Victoria, you aren't."

Victoria threw her weight hard against him, shoving him backward over the carcass of the buck. In the instant he went tumbling to the floor, she turned and yanked on the leather flap sealing the doorway. She opened it enough to slither out.

"No!" he shouted. "Come back here!"

Victoria pushed through the waist-deep powder snow that had drifted against the entrance. She was so desperate to get away that she ignored the chill of the snow on her bare feet and the icy wind that cut right through her. By the time she made it to the ledge, Jarred was pushing his way out after her.

"No, don't!" he screamed.

The pulsing of the chopper's blades was loud and getting louder. Looking frantically up the ridge line, she saw the dark spot in the sky moving toward her. It couldn't have been much more than half a mile away. She began running along the ledge, waving her arms and shouting, knowing that Jarred was right behind her.

She hadn't gone twenty yards, struggling through the knee-deep snow, before he tackled her, knocking her to the ground. Victoria fell facedown in the snow, the weight of his body crushing her. Instantly he rolled with her against the overhanging rock beside them, pinning her there.

Victoria gasped for air, crying out futilely as he held her down in the snowdrift. About then the aircraft roared overhead, no more than a few hundred feet above them. Fighting against his weight, she listened to the engine, praying that the sound wouldn't fade, that they had been seen, that the chopper would circle back.

It didn't. It continued to move on down the ridge line, the pulsing of the blades growing fainter and fainter. Without adrenaline, her body gave up, and all the fight went out of her. She felt helpless, spent.

"Come on, Victoria," he said, rolling off her and standing up. "You'll freeze if you stay out here. We have to go back inside."

She didn't move. She wanted to die, to give up.

"Victoria!" he urged firmly.

She began to sob, suddenly too weak to do anything else. Jarred reached down and, taking her by the waistband of her jeans, lifted her to her feet. She was limp as a rag doll as he carried her back to the cave. Her teeth were chattering by the time they got inside. He set her down by the fire and wrapped her in her blanket, reaching under it to rub her icy feet.

Victoria stared at the ceiling. Tears continued to roll down her cheeks, though she'd stopped sobbing. She felt doomed.

Jarred didn't admonish her. He didn't say anything. Eventually he went off into the depths of the cave. After about ten minutes, he returned with a steaming tin cup filled with tea.

"Drink this," he said.

Victoria sat up and took the cup from him, inhaling the aroma before taking a sip. She drank as fast as she was able. When she'd finished, she handed back the empty cup and lay down again.

She didn't look at Jarred the entire time, nor did he speak to her. She rolled on to her side, her back to him, and gazed at the fire. Then, after a minute, she heard him get up and walk away.

IT ONLY TOOK Jarred a short while to finish with the buck. When he'd butchered it and readied the hide for tanning, all that remained was to dispose of the carcass and clean up the mess. As he worked, the helicopter came back, making another circuit of the valley. He was almost sure they hadn't been spotted, though he could have been wrong. He listened to the engine, glancing over at Victoria where she still lay by the fire. He saw her lift her head as the sound of the aircraft became stronger, but she put it back down again as though she no longer cared.

It had infuriated him that she had run out like that, nearly compromising him and the home he'd worked so hard to keep hidden from the outside world. It proved she couldn't be trusted. But why she'd done it today, and not the day before, he couldn't understand. What had changed?

Of course, she'd been upset when he told her she couldn't leave until after the winter was over. So maybe that was it. Maybe the winter seemed too long for her to be alone with him.

Angry as he was with her, in a way Jarred felt sorry for her, too. She was afraid. Not everyone could handle the loneliness, the isolation. He knew now that bringing her here had been a big mistake.

Things had seemed a lot different the past few days. At first having a woman in the cave had been troubling, but it was beginning to feel better all the time.

The night before, when he'd bathed, he'd gotten aroused, knowing that under her blanket she was naked. And when he'd awakened that morning, knowing she was just in the next room, he'd become aroused again. He'd imagined himself making love to her, taking her because he wanted to. It had been like that with some of the girls he'd had. Of course, with Tracey it had been different. She had loved him and they had planned on getting married. Victoria was not like that.

Just then the helicopter passed overhead, the throbbing of its engine so loud that the window vibrated. Victoria didn't move, didn't even react to the sound. He knew she was still crying and, though he was ashamed to admit it, her sorrow made his heart ache.

AFTER AN HOUR'S REST, Victoria hadn't gotten all of her strength back. The tea had warmed her, but Jarred hadn't offered her any food.

Deciding she owed him no courtesies, Victoria went to the larder and helped herself to an assortment of food. Despite her craving for something new, she wasn't about to speak to Jarred. So, she gathered some nuts and berries, jerky and an apple. As she made her way back to the fire, she glanced at him. They briefly made eye contact, neither saying a word.

She had heard him leave the cave earlier, when he'd dragged the carcass of the buck outside. She had no idea where he'd taken it. He'd cleaned up and was sitting cross-legged under the light of the window, working on something, though she couldn't tell what.

Victoria kept her back to him as she ate, wanting to make sure he knew he was being deprived of her company. If he was going to behave like a brute, he would have to do without her friendship.

As the day wore on, she lounged by the fire, resting and napping. Jarred silently worked at whatever it was he'd found to occupy himself. Neither of them spoke, nor did they look at each other much. Victoria rapidly became bored.

As much as she would have loved to read one of his books, she was afraid that might be pushing things—considering how upset he'd gotten when he'd learned about her snooping. Better she spend the winter in silence than ask to borrow a book.

Jarred had had a lot more practice at this solitude business than she'd had and would have no trouble outlasting her silence. He could virtually ignore her and go on as he had the past fifteen years. For her, days with nothing to do but sleep and eat would get excruciatingly boring pretty fast. What it meant, of course, was that she had to get the hell out of there. If not by air, then by foot.

In the middle of the afternoon, she took a nap. When she awoke, she was startled to see Jarred sitting next to her, gazing into the fire. He looked at her and smiled faintly.

"I have a present for you," he said. Then he handed her a pair of moccasins. They were fur-lined and looked perfectly wonderful.

Disconcerted by his gesture, she sat up and looked into his eyes. "You made these for me?"

"Yes."

"Thank you. They're very nice."

"When I rubbed your feet, I got an idea what size they were. I think they'll fit. Try them."

Victoria pulled her feet from under the blanket and slipped on the moccasins. They were perfect.

"How are they?" he asked.

"Just right."

The look in his eye told her he was pleased with himself. "I'll make a special dinner tonight," he said. "I don't have a lot of butane, but we should have a special meal every once in a while."

"Butane? Is that how you boiled the water for the tea?"

"Yes, I have a single-burner camp stove in the storage room. And lots of canned food. I have beef stew and chili and lots of vegetables. Does that interest you?"

She nodded.

"Tonight we can have fresh venison," he said. "I can heat up some corn and green beans. Would you like that?"

She nodded again. In spite of his generosity, she wasn't about to let him off the hook so easily.

"Jarred, I hate to bring up a sore subject..." she paused for a moment. "I'm really upset by what happened this morning," she continued. "We're going to have to talk about it."

Then he did something totally unexpected. He reached out and took her hand, rubbing the back of it with his thumb. Victoria was so startled that she didn't say anything. Then she noticed how strong his hand was. His fingers were almost like an artist's.

There was a gleam of awareness in his eyes. He remained silent and so she quickly pulled her hand back.

"All right," he said, ignoring her rejection. "If you want to talk, we can. But let's have dinner first. I always feel better when my stomach is full."

"Okay," she said. "If that's what you want, we can talk after dinner."

"I just want to say one thing now. I hope I didn't hurt you when I knocked you down in the snow. And I hope you aren't too sad."

"I *am* sad."

"Then we'll talk about that," he said. "Later. The rest of the meat has to be smoked before it spoils."

He got to his feet and looked down at her with a measure of satisfaction. She sensed his feeling of triumph.

"It's snowing," he said, tossing his head toward the entrance to the cave.

She looked over at the window, alarm going through her. Sure enough, in the late afternoon light, she saw snowflakes drifting by the windowpane.

8

JARRED WAS still smoking the venison she'd helped him slice only minutes before. They'd worked well together, she carving up the meat so that he could take it over to the hollowed out spot at the rear of the cave he used as an oven.

They had labored in companionable silence for the most part. Lingering at the edge of the silence was the increased sexual tension between them. No matter how many times Victoria ran it back through her head, she couldn't dismiss the fact that he had every intention of keeping her there for the winter.

The worst part was, she hadn't come up with a strategy for handling things from here on out. She was still indignant about his heavy-handedness in keeping her from signaling the chopper. Nevertheless, she knew it was in her interest to temper the hostility between them.

So where did that leave her? If she was friendly, Jarred might well construe it as a come-on. If she was hostile, he could retaliate. Her best bet might be to appeal to his reason. However, without his trust, she had little hope of convincing him to accept her views on the situation.

By the time he'd finished smoking the meat, it was nearly dark and they had to light the lantern. Jarred got out the venison steaks and began slowly roasting them over the fire. Victoria wandered over to the window and watched the snow steadily fall.

When she looked back into the cave, she saw that Jarred had been watching her. He quickly lowered his eyes to the vegetables he was cooking on the butane stove he'd set up.

She set the table while he finished cooking. Then he disappeared into the small sleeping cave for several minutes. When he returned, he'd put on a blue and gray wool plaid shirt. He'd also combed his hair and smoothed his beard. A definite transformation had taken place.

Victoria didn't say anything, because it was fairly clear what he was thinking. He'd already seen her naked. He'd stared at her legs. He'd taken her hand. And he had to have noticed how those things had affected her. Now he was ready for the grand seduction. The only question was whether he'd accept her rejection, or force her to accommodate him. She knew she'd have to play things out very, very carefully.

"Since it's our first real dinner," he said, "I decided I should try to look a little better than usual."

Victoria was more conscious than ever of the vibrations between them. How should she respond? Should she say something? It seemed best not to say anything.

Jarred finished cooking the food. He put it on the table and Victoria began dishing it onto the plates. Before she could even comment on how good everything smelled, Jarred abruptly left the table. "Why don't I light a candle?" he said. "It's not often I have a woman to dinner."

Victoria swallowed hard. She decided right then that her best bet might be to be friendly. Cordial, but not so blatant as to give him the wrong idea. Within moments he was back from the supply room, lighting the candle before sitting down.

"How's that?" he asked, looking pleased with himself.

"Your resourcefulness never ceases to amaze."

"All that's missing is the white tablecloth and wine," he said with a laugh.

"I thought you'd be bringing that out next."

A sad smile touched his lips. Jarred combed through his beard with his fingers. "You know, I've never tasted wine. I've had beer. Never wine."

They looked at each other and, in spite of all her resolve, Victoria felt a surge of compassion for him, for all he'd missed. While she had a strong desire to reach out to him, she recognized how dangerous it could be to act on it.

They began eating. Everything tasted heavenly. "You didn't scavenge all this, did you?"

Jarred shook his head. "No."

"But I suppose I'm not supposed to ask where you got it."

"I have a friend," he admitted. "Somebody I've known for a long time."

"Macky Bean?"

Jarred grew quiet. He looked very uncomfortable. Then he said, "Promise me you won't ever repeat his name to anyone."

"I promise. But tell me about him. Please."

Jarred chewed, swallowed, then took a long drink of water. He seemed reluctant, as if he was having a difficult time deciding whether or not he should reveal the story.

"Macky was my father's best friend. I'd only seen him a few times before I took off for the mountains. He's got a shack at the end of an old logging road about seven or eight miles from here. That first year I knew I'd never get through the winter without help, so I went down to Macky's place.

"He was drunk when I got there, and he got all emotional. Macky's a recluse, a loner, and he also drinks a lot. He and my dad were in Vietnam together. Macky was holding my father in his arms when he died. He tells me the story every time he gets drunk."

"He gives you these supplies?"

"Yes, I go down once or twice a year. It's not that I'm all that close to Macky, because I'm not. But it means a lot to him to help me because of his feelings for my father. And the supplies do make my life a lot easier."

"Aren't you afraid he might give you away, if only inadvertently?"

"I'm more worried about him dying, to tell you the truth. Keeping me going has been a crusade for him. Sometimes I think it's what keeps him alive. He does everything in his power to help me, including stealing library books. I bring them back for him to return," Jarred said with a guilty smile. "They are off the library shelves for months at a time."

"That explains a lot," she said. "You've read more than most people who have college educations, I bet."

"I do read a lot, especially in the winter."

"Why did you hide this other side from me?"

"Talking with you isn't as easy as you think, Victoria. Even sitting here now, looking at you across this table, seems very strange. I don't speak to anyone but myself for months on end. Other than Macky, you're the only person who's ever come here."

"Then Macky's the only person you have a relationship with?"

"Macky's the only human being I've spoken to in all these years."

"You must cherish the hours you're together."

"Old Macky is a great guy, I have to admit. Worries about me like you wouldn't believe. One fall he had a whole pile of skin magazines waiting for me. I brought them back to the cave. It was torture looking at them. So after a few weeks I burned them."

Jarred drained the last of the water. She looked into his eyes and realized that having her around was torture for him, too.

It was true that she wasn't exactly here of her own free will; it was also true that he'd saved her life. And since she'd been in the cave, she'd turned his existence upside down. Being around a woman—any woman— had to be difficult for him.

He was undoubtedly oblivious to her misgivings because his face was much more animated and relaxed than at any time since she'd met him.

And his newfound loquaciousness was a real surprise. It seemed that once he got to talking, it all came spilling out. At least he was less guarded than before.

"You're a very good cook," she said, taking another bite. "The meat is perfect."

He grinned. "Sometimes I wish I could fix different things. I dream about pies. Macky gave me a sack of flour once. I tried to make a crust. When I added the water, everything turned to mud. I asked him how to make a pie crust the next time I saw him. He said he'd buy me a pie. Then he forgot about it. One time he brought me a half a dozen stale donuts. I ate them anyway."

"A stale donut doesn't sound half-bad."

"I guess I sound like a babbling fool," he said. "Sorry if I'm running off at the mouth."

"You don't have a lot of opportunities for conversation."

She detected something in his eyes—a thought about her that likely would have made her blush if he had expressed it. She observed him take her in and Victoria began feeling uneasy again. Initially she had feared the beast in Jarred. Now she was beginning to fear the effect of the man.

Jarred sat back in his chair. He stared at her with his luminous eyes. Emotionally traumatic as this experience was for her, Victoria knew it had to be even more so for him.

"I like you, Victoria," he said, folding his arms over his broad chest. "I know you want to talk about what happened this morning. Before we do, I wanted you to know that."

His utter sincerity touched her. She smiled. "Thank you. I appreciate your saying that."

"And it's not because you're the first woman I've talked to in years. It's because I think you're nice. I do."

"Are you sure about your reasons for that, Jarred?"

He frowned. "What are you saying? That I can't know how I feel because you're the first woman I've been around in a long time?"

"No, of course you know how you feel. I'm not criticizing you, I'm just trying to explain."

He looked displeased. "I don't like it when you explain things. Living like I do might make me a little strange, but I'm no fool."

"If I hurt your feelings, I apologize," she said.

Jarred said nothing. It seemed as though he might be withdrawing into his shell.

"Listen," she said. "Can I be blunt with you?"

He waited.

"I want you to go back with me. Back to town."

Jarred sat in a stony silence, his face expressionless.

"Don't close your mind to it, Jarred," she pleaded.

He remained impassive.

"At least discuss it with me. Please."

"I'll never go back."

"Why?"

"Because this is my life and there is nothing for me in Edgar."

"Jarred, no charges were brought against you because of what happened to Todd. If you were to return now, you wouldn't have any problems with the law. Most people recognize what you did was in self-defense."

"I know that. Macky told me. I'm not afraid of the law."

"Then why won't you go back? You're still young. You have a whole life ahead of you."

"I just want to be left alone."

"I don't understand why."

"You don't have to."

He seemed so determined. She shouldn't have been surprised. If fifteen years of loneliness hadn't driven him out of the mountains, how could she hope to convince him in a single evening? She stared at the flickering candle, feeling a terrible sadness. When she looked up, she found him staring at her intensely.

"It's not your problem, Victoria."

"I'd like to help you. I can't, if you won't let me."

"You're the one who needs help," he said. "And that's what I've been doing the past few days. We're in my world, not yours."

"Yes, I owe you my life, I know that."

"That's not the point. It's a question of survival. For that, you need me, and you need this place."

"I don't want to be here, any more than you want to go back."

"Because of me?" he asked.

"Because of a lot of things."

"Tell me what."

Victoria agonized. How could she explain? There was a whole world out there, her world. "I'm not here by choice," she said finally. "Do you understand that?"

Jarred watched her. She stared at the candle for a long time. Whenever she glanced up, he was waiting with a hurt look in his eyes.

"I would have let you signal the helicopter if I could have," he said.

"Would you really?"

"It wouldn't have pleased me," he admitted.

"You see, Jarred, there's our problem."

He folded his arms over his chest, leaning back in his chair. She had been brutally frank, even at the risk of hurting him, but it was necessary. She had to make him understand her feelings.

"Do you have a boyfriend?" he asked suddenly.

Although surprised by the question, she saw the progression of his thoughts. He was being frank about what was on his mind, too. "I did," she replied honestly. "There's nobody at the moment."

"I thought maybe that might be why you don't want to be here with me."

"Yes, I know that's what you were thinking." She looked down at her hands. "But that's not the reason."

"I don't get it," he said.

She was growing more and more distressed. "Let's talk about something else."

After an uncomfortable silence, he said, "Tell me about your life. I don't know anything about you except that you're at a university."

She was glad for the change the subject, grateful he'd let her off the hook. "I grew up on my grandmother's ranch in Siskiyou County, in Northern California," she said. "I'm no city girl."

"I didn't think you were. I've only been to Seattle a few times, enough to know it wasn't like Edgar. The people there were different."

"I guess my heart's still in Scotts Valley."

"What is your family like?"

She told him how her grandmother had raised her after her parents' car had gone off an icy road, killing them both. She related how, in spite of that tragedy, she'd enjoyed a happy childhood. Growing up on a

ranch, she'd learned self-reliance and the importance
of hard work. Since her grandmother's death, the ranch
had been hers, she told him, though for the past several years it had been leased out.

"Do you go back there often?" he asked.

"It's been a few years. When I drove up the interstate
to come here, I passed within twenty miles of it. Made
me a little homesick, to be honest."

"Do you miss your grandmother?"

Victoria's eyes shimmered as she related how close
they had been, how she'd adored the old woman. All
the talk of family made her sentimental, accentuating
their isolation, how cut off she was from the world. She
apologized when a tear ran down her cheek. "I don't
know how you've lived alone all this time," she said,
wiping her eyes.

"I'm not alone now, and neither are you."

His words set off a warning signal and she looked at
him uncertainly. He fixed his gaze on her.

"Did you love your boyfriend?" he asked, his question betraying his train of thought.

"I suppose I thought I did. Evidently not enough."

"What happened?"

Jarred, she could see, really wanted to know about
her love life. So much of who a person was was re-
vealed by whom they chose to be with.

For her, men had always been a mixed bag. She'd
gone through high school madly in love with a guy who
cared for somebody else. Then, at college, it seemed
there were too many guys and that they were all after
the same thing. The college men weren't like the cowboys she'd grown up with. They made her uncomfort-

able in a different sort of way. She'd dated and had had a couple of intimate relationships. None of the men had been what she was looking for.

By the time she'd made it to graduate school, she figured she pretty well had men in perspective. During her first two years she had dated Randall McPherson, a graduate student in chemistry. He was a decent, unassuming person, serious about his work and willing to share his life. Victoria thought that was what she needed and wanted. They'd lived together the last six months before Randall was awarded his Ph.D. and took a teaching job at Cal Poly.

"When Randall left Berkeley he wanted me to go with him," she told Jarred. "He wanted us to get married."

"But you didn't?"

"I wasn't sure. I wanted to finish my own doctoral studies, so I stayed behind. Randall thought we'd get together later. The separation demonstrated to me it wasn't the relationship I desired."

"Maybe you didn't love him after all," Jarred said.

"Maybe I didn't."

They regarded each other in silence again. Victoria could sense the wheels turning.

There were a few kernels of corn left on her plate and she scraped them up, then put down her fork. "That was a delicious dinner," she said. "Thank you."

"It's the best I've had in a long time," he said. "Not because of the food."

Victoria got up. "Since you cooked, I'll clean up."

Jarred got to his feet, as well.

"Go sit by the fire and take it easy," she said. "Next time I'll cook and you can clean up."

"Is that the way you did it with Randall?"

She nodded, then turned away.

It only took her a few minutes to do the dishes, carrying the lantern with her to the large tub where the water was kept. Jarred watched her from his rocking chair by the fire. When she'd finished putting the dishes away, she walked over to him.

He looked up at her. "I hope our conversation didn't make you too sad," he said.

"Do I look sad?"

He nodded. "Yes."

It was strange how direct they were with each other. Normally communication was layered with so many levels of meaning. With Randall, as with everybody else she'd known, the intended message was usually in the subtext. The only other person she'd known who'd spoken so directly from the heart had been her grandmother.

Jarred got up and stood before her. He seemed so large to her when they were face-to-face. She'd gotten used to the beard and the long hair—they did not detract from his appeal.

He reached out unexpectedly and took hold of her shoulders. "I don't want you to be sad, Victoria," he said.

"It's nothing. The past few days have made me emotional." She smiled nervously, unable to ignore the warmth of his hands through her shirt. "Maybe the clunk on the head is part of it."

He took her chin in his hand and examined her face. "It's looking much better. Not so swollen as before. If you'd seen all the blood when I pulled you out of the creek, you would have been shocked. I assumed you were dead."

He brushed her cheek with the back of his fingers and Victoria shivered. She felt such strong vibrations from him, yet she had the impression that he was restraining himself. It made her nervous. She tried to pull away but Jarred wouldn't let her go. "Did it upset you when I said I liked you a while ago?"

She shook her head, feeling his power, his will, and his desire. There was such intensity on his face that it frightened her, and compelled her.

He lightly ran his fingers back through her hair. "You're very beautiful, Victoria. I like to touch you. You're so soft."

She bit her lip. Part of her wanted to embrace him, to connect, to be at one with him and his loneliness; another part of her was terrified of where it might lead.

"I looked at your mouth when you were sleeping," he said, his voice deeper, sexier than ever before. "I wanted to kiss it. I didn't think it was right because I didn't know you. But now I do. I want to kiss you even more."

Jarred didn't seem to notice her trembling. He had hold of her upper arms. His fingers sank into her flesh and she could feel his strength and warmth. "Don't think about that," she murmured. "It's not a good idea."

For an answer, he pulled her toward him, as effortlessly as if she were a child. She felt as though he could lift her off her feet if he wished. Victoria was mesmerized. With the light of the fire playing on his face, she felt helpless.

Jarred lowered his head and gently touched his lips to hers. It was a tender kiss, powerful in its restraint, enthralling in its promise.

Victoria didn't resist. She let him kiss her, marveling at the feel of the mustache and beard enveloping her mouth like a soft web. His lips were moist and sensuous. And as he slipped his tongue into her mouth, he gathered her against him, enclosing her in the circle of his arms.

The tingling in her breasts and the bulge in his loins awoke her to what was happening. He was kissing her deeply now, and she knew she couldn't let herself give into it. That could only lead to disaster. She forced herself to break free of the kiss.

"No," she murmured breathlessly. "We can't, Jarred."

He began kissing her neck, ignoring her protest. Fear welled in her. She managed to get her hands between their bodies and pushed against his chest as hard as she could.

"No!" she cried. It was virtually a shout.

Jarred released her so suddenly that she fell back a step. He seemed shocked, perplexed. "What's the matter!"

"I don't want you kissing me!" she said, her voice quavering.

"Why? What's wrong?" He reached out and took her wrist, his face filled with consternation, confusion.

She jerked her arm free and backed farther away. And when he took a step toward her, she turned and darted to the far side of the fire. "Leave me alone!" she screamed.

"Victoria, what did I do?" he pleaded. "I only wanted to kiss you. I thought you wanted me to."

"I didn't!"

"But . . . I thought—"

"You were wrong, Jarred!" Her heart was pounding wildly and she felt as threatened as when Steve Parnell had come at her in his drunken rage. "Just stay away from me. Please!"

His expression turned from shock to anger. "I only did what I thought you wanted."

"I'm sorry if I misled you. I guess I was feeling compassion and you misunderstood that for something else."

He shook his head. "That's not what happened. You're afraid of something else."

She took a deep breath, trying to calm down. "Well, it was a misunderstanding. It was my fault. Don't try to kiss me again. Really."

He glared at her, his displeasure evident. Several long minutes passed. Finally he spoke. "I'm going to bed." He strode toward the entrance to the sleeping chamber.

"Jarred," she called.

He stopped. "What?"

"I'm sorry. It's not your fault, it's mine."

"Why didn't you just say you didn't like me? It would have been better."

"It's not true. I do like you. Just not that way."

He considered the remark, but only for a moment. Without further comment, he disappeared into the adjoining chamber.

9

FOR A WHILE after Jarred had left her, Victoria stood by the crackling fire, feeling so empty and defeated—so lost.

Any hope she'd had was gone. Jarred hated her now. She'd rejected him, wounded his pride, and she couldn't even begin to imagine how things would be between them from this point on. Everything was so confused.

She sat down after a while, hugging her knees to her chest, wishing she'd never left Berkeley, that she'd never gotten into this mess. It could have been worse, though. Jarred might not have stopped, he might not have accepted no for an answer.

She knew it was entirely possible that the next time he felt desire for her, it would end differently. They were, as he'd reminded her, in *his* world. He was lord and master here, and she was completely dependent upon him.

Whether Jarred had mistreated her or not, the potential was there. How could she hope to keep him at bay forever? And he wasn't the only problem. She had learned the hard way that she was every bit as capable of losing control as he. She hadn't resisted when he'd kissed her, and she'd gotten aroused before she'd finally stopped him. That was proof of how fragile the situation was.

Within weeks, if not days, they would be intimate, whether out of mutual weakness or his unwillingness to stay away from her, she didn't know. The outcome was inevitable, unless, of course, she got out of there before something happened.

She would have to get far enough from the cave that she could flag down the helicopter without compromising Jarred. And if the chopper didn't come back, she would just have to walk out of the mountains. There was no other choice.

It had snowed off and on all day, but if it cleared by morning, she would go then. Jarred had insisted she couldn't make it down the mountain alone. Since the winter snows were only beginning, she was certain he had exaggerated.

He would undoubtedly try to prevent her, so she would have to leave early, before dawn broke, before he was up. She went to bed then, praying it would be clear in the morning and that the helicopter crew hadn't abandoned their search. She slept fitfully. From time to time her eyes would pop open and she would look toward the window to make sure she hadn't overslept.

When she finally decided it was time, she got up, lit a candle and went to the window to check the weather. The snow seemed to have stopped.

She quietly rummaged through the storeroom, looking for extra clothes. Lacking a heavy coat, she hoped she would stay warm by layering her clothing. Her biggest concern was her feet. The moccasins Jarred had made were fine for padding around the cave, but hardly suitable in the snow. She could lash skins over them just as Jarred had over his boots, creating an additional layer of insulation.

She dressed quickly. From fur-lined patches of buckskin and leather thongs she fashioned a hat and crude mittens. The entire process of dressing took longer than she had anticipated. By the time she had gathered a few handfuls of nuts, dried berries and an apple, the sky was already showing the first signs of light.

She extinguished the candle and glanced toward the sleeping cave, knowing how angry Jarred would be when he discovered that she'd gone. She would have liked to have left him a note. However, the only writing materials were by his bed. It probably didn't matter, though. Her actions would speak for themselves.

Stepping outside, she was greeted with a blast of cold air. The wind cut right through her. She looked at the sky that was just beginning to turn gray and knew that snow was in the air. Victoria knew she was taking a terrible risk. A wave of doubt went through her. The alternative was to spend the entire winter alone with Jarred.

Taking a deep breath, she began slogging through the huge snowdrift at the entrance of the cave. She made her way to the ledge and looked down. Far below, in the murky gloom of early light, she could see the valley. The meadow where she had paraded around to catch Jarred's attention was barely visible. She would head for it and, with a little luck, she might even be able to find her own clothes.

Fortunately her trek would take her downhill. Considering the way she was clothed, she knew that not having to expend energy in climbing could make all the difference.

The cold was bitter, nearly unbearable, with the wind chill robbing her of body heat. The makeshift boots afforded almost no traction and she had trouble keeping her footing on the icy rocks. Trudging through deep snow was exhausting, so she paused for rest where she could. The faintness of the light didn't help, and she fell several times, once badly bruising her hip.

After a while, the slope leveled out and she was able to make better time. But as daylight came, so did some flurries of snow. She looked up at the leaden sky and groaned. She would be in for a rough time. The bad weather would ground the helicopter, which meant she would have to walk back to civilization under her own power. The odds had suddenly turned against her.

She had descended perhaps a thousand feet when she decided to take a breather. She squeezed into a crevice in the rocks to protect herself from the wind. The cold was rapidly sapping her energy. It was clear that she hadn't fully regained her strength and the challenge would have been formidable enough without the handicap of a weakened body. If only the storm had waited one more day!

About the time she rallied enough to resume her descent, the crystalline morning air was broken by the sound of her name echoing across the valley. Jarred was calling to her. Even at this distance she could detect the anxiety in his voice.

She steeled herself against the rush of sentimentality, knowing she had to press ahead, no matter what the cost. Every minute brought her closer to the point when she would run out of energy. Once that happened, it was over.

On the lower portions of the mountain the drifts were deeper. Several times she plunged into snow above her waist and had to fight her way out—a struggle that used up valuable energy. She was miles from the nearest road, and making it to civilization was beginning to seem an insurmountable challenge. Her strength was deserting her, her legs were turning to rubber. The thigh high snow seemed like quicksand and more of it was falling, swirling down from the sky and threatening to bury her. Victoria had to fight down the panic that welled up from time to time.

Every few steps she had to stop, her chest heaving, her body close to collapse, the hopelessness of her situation impossible to deny. She was tempted to lie down to rest but that meant certain death.

Struggling, she wedged herself in another crevice. She ate a few nuts, then some snow, knowing that dehydration was a danger. Victoria only allowed herself a brief respite. She resolved to go on until she was spent. At least she'd gotten far enough from the cave that even if she didn't make it, she wouldn't have compromised Jarred.

Gathering herself, she recalled that her grandmother's favorite expression was "Never give up." So she slogged along, muttering the words over and over. "Never give up. Never give up."

Her legs turned to lead. Every step became a battle. Finally she sank waist-deep into a snowdrift and collapsed. It was over. She let go, staring toward the heavens and the swirling snow.

A strange peacefulness settled over her as she contemplated her death. Her body relaxed and she closed her eyes to go to sleep for the last time.

The next thing Victoria knew she was brusquely being lifted by the shoulders. She opened her eyes, startled to see Jarred. His face showed fear and maybe anger. His beard was frosted white. Vapors were issuing from his mouth and he looked like a vengeful god.

"Victoria, why did you run away?" he growled. "They won't come in a storm. What were you thinking of?"

She had no answers. She longed to lie back and sleep. Then he shook her so hard that it hurt.

"Wake up, Victoria. You can't stay here. We have to go back."

"I can't," she said. "I'm too tired."

Jarred didn't argue. He started dragging her to a nearby stand of pine. Leaning her against a log, he hollowed out a place in the snow, wrapped her in a fur-lined buckskin blanket he was carrying, and eased her into the snow cave. He wedged in beside her, and wrapped his arm around her.

By then Victoria realized he wasn't going to let her die. She pressed her face against his wet beard and began to cry. Jarred held her close, and between the blanket and his body heat, she felt almost able to fight the cold. The refuge was only temporary, though.

"For somebody who teaches college, you're pretty dumb," he said. "It's going to be a lot harder going up the mountain than coming down."

"I'll never make it."

"You have to. We can't last outside through the night. It's a bad storm and it could go on for days. We have to get back to the cave right away."

"I can't, Jarred," she said. "I know I can't. Just leave me. Save yourself. Go on."

He smiled, as though she'd said the stupidest thing he'd ever heard. "It's your turn to cook dinner. You don't expect me to make it two times in a row, do you?"

She smiled weakly. "How can you joke at a time like this?"

"It's easy. The most important time to joke is when things look bad," he said. "I was mauled by a bear once and bleeding all over the place. I knew I'd die if I didn't get to the cave. So while I crawled back, I told myself jokes. Once or twice I even laughed."

She shook her head. "You're amazing."

"Good," he said. "You're giving compliments. That means you aren't ready to die yet." He touched her cheek with his fingers and smiled.

"But I can't walk up that mountain, Jarred. I really can't. So don't waste your time and energy on me."

"If you can't walk, I will have to carry you. I did it before."

"Yes, but there wasn't three feet of snow on the ground then."

"Don't argue. It only uses energy. First, we'll eat. Later, we will start back."

Jarred produced a pouch with nuts, berries and jerky. They ate from the pouch and also had some more snow from the walls of their shelter. Victoria felt halfway rejuvenated.

Jarred refused to be dissuaded, so she summoned her willpower. They clambered out of the snow cave and into the storm. It was snowing so heavily that Victoria felt completely disoriented. Jarred steered her toward the mountainside that was practically invisible in the blizzard.

He picked a route that was comparatively easy. Victoria was able to walk for a while, though when the terrain began to grow steeper, she faltered. Jarred picked her up and threw her over his shoulder.

After twenty minutes of climbing and carrying Victoria, he was perspiring heavily and puffs of vapor were spewing from his mouth with each breath. Finally, he set her down at the base of a boulder and dropped beside her.

"This is impossible," she said. "If you waste your energy this way, you'll die, too. Go on without me, Jarred. Just leave me here."

"No," he said stubbornly. "We will both make it."

They'd only gone a tiny fraction of the way back up the mountain. At this rate it would take all day and into the night to reach the cave.

"If you can walk for a while, I'll get my strength back," he said.

"I'll try."

They began their ascent once more. Jarred had picked a route that was steep and rocky, but had less snow on the ground. Each step was agonizing. Victoria gave it her all, but after another hundred yards, she was spent. Again Jarred heaved her over his shoulder, resting every dozen yards or so to take a few breaths.

She could tell he was becoming exhausted. It would have been a difficult enough climb on his own. Somehow he'd managed to give her a spark of hope, when for hours she'd had none.

Halfway up the mountain, Jarred built them another snow cave. They curled up together, trying to conserve their body heat and rebuild their energies. They ate the last of the food he had brought and then took a few minutes to rest.

She watched as he stared out at the blizzard, his eyes hard with determination. She didn't understand why he'd made such a sacrifice. There was no question he'd risked, potentially even endangered, his life for her. Shivering, she pressed her face against his shoulder. Jarred nuzzled her forehead.

"Why did you leave?" he asked. "Was it because I kissed you, or because I yelled at you? Were you afraid of me?"

She shook her head. "I was afraid of the situation."

"I don't understand."

"It doesn't matter. We'll never make it back anyway."

"Yes, we will!" he insisted angrily. "Both of us!"

There was no point in arguing. Jarred Wilde had long since proven he was a man of tremendous will. He'd conquered every challenge he'd faced.

After a few more minutes of rest, he announced it was time to go. He helped her out of the snow cave and asked if she was able to walk. Victoria said she would try.

She made it farther than she expected, though at times he had to half carry her. When her legs finally gave out, he put her over his shoulder and resumed the climb. His determination was relentless. It was obvious, however, that he was weakening. His breathing was labored, his gait unsteady. When they came to a rocky escarpment, he had to drag her from ledge to ledge. Once, when he lost his footing, Victoria grabbed his hand, steadying him long enough to help him regain his balance.

Dropping down beside her to catch his breath, he gazed out at the blinding snow. "I think I'll make you cook dinner for a week," he said, panting.

"I guess I owe you that much."

"Did your grandmother spank you when you were little?"

"No, but she had a real sharp tongue."

"I may give you your first thrashing when we get back," he said. "This is not my idea of fun." Jarred cuffed her jaw, then kissed her cheek, his icy lips feeling brittle on her frozen skin. Still, his affection warmed her.

Her mind was still sharp enough to see the irony in the situation. She had run away to escape him and the sexual threat he posed, and now it was his affection that was bolstering her lagging spirits.

"It will be dark in an hour, maybe less," he said, struggling to his feet. "We must make it to the cave before then."

"How much farther?"

"A quarter of the way. The hardest quarter. We will make it, Victoria."

With Jarred carrying her they made it to the top of the first escarpment. Darkness began falling and he stumbled frequently. For Victoria, it was a struggle to stay conscious. Sometimes she would fade out, only to wake up on the ground with Jarred slapping her face. The last time she awoke, it was practically dark. Jarred was breathing so hard he looked as though he'd just run a marathon. His jaw was slack and the fire in his eyes was gone.

"It's no use," she said, barely having the energy to speak. "Just go."

His response was to struggle to his feet. Peering up at him in the swirling snow, she thought he'd finally accepted her plea, that this was their last farewell. Instead of stumbling away, he grabbed her by the collar and began dragging her across the icy rocks, his legs giving out every once in a while, forcing him to collapse beside her. Then he would fight his way to his feet again, and drag her a few more yards.

After that, she faded in and out of consciousness. She'd feel the rocks and snow on her backside as he dragged her limp body over the uneven ground. Her last thought before blacking out for good was that when they made it to the cave, she would probably be dead.

THE DARKNESS was complete. Even the snow was invisible. Jarred had been over this ridge so often that every boulder was familiar. They were within a hundred yards of the entrance to the cave. It might have been a hundred miles, given how absolutely enervated he was. To crawl there alone seemed an impossible task. Still, he would rather die than give up his struggle to save Victoria. She was near death and all that could save her now was to get her to the cave and get her warm.

Jarred was on his hands and knees, pulling her body behind him. Rock by rock, he inched forward. At last they reached the mouth of the cave. Snow had drifted over the door. He began clawing it away with his hands, knowing that every minute counted. At a certain point, Victoria's heart would simply stop.

Finally he made it to the door and pushed his way in. Then, crawling back, he grabbed Victoria by the collar and got her inside, collapsing where he'd dropped the buck. He lay panting with his cheek against the cold rock floor.

The fire had long since gone out and the cave was pitch-black. Fortunately he knew every inch of it. He made his way to the table where there were matches and a candle. His numb fingers were so stiff that he had trouble striking the match. Finally he got the stub of a candle lit. He staggered back to Victoria. The snow was swirling in the doorway, so he closed the flap of leather as best he could and pulled her to the pallet. Covering her with the bearskin, he slapped her face a few times, hoping it wasn't too late, that she still had some life in her.

He could tell she was breathing even though she didn't respond. "Victoria!" he shouted. "Wake up!"

Her lids fluttered and she looked at him, a dazed expression on her face. Unable to contain his joy, he kissed her mouth, her nose and cheeks.

"We made it!" he wheezed, his eyes flooding. "We're home!"

She moaned, and began shivering violently. Jarred went to make a fire. Back at her side, he discovered her awake and staring at the ceiling.

"Are we all right?" she muttered, when he put his face over hers so she could see him.

"Yes, we're safe."

Her eyes filled with tears, running down her cheeks. "I'm so cold."

"You'll warm up soon. I have to get you out of these wet clothes."

She was silent as he stripped her. Once he had her wrapped in a dry, fur-lined blanket, she seemed more comfortable.

"We have to eat and drink," he said. Then he stumbled over to the food bins, gathered a variety of things, as well as a cup of water, and took them to where Victoria lay shivering under her blanket. "Here," he said, offering her the cup and helping her lift her head. "Drink this."

When he fed her bits of food, she summoned enough energy to chew and swallow. Jarred eagerly ate, as well.

Once Victoria was revived, he began stripping off his own wet clothing. He'd been so concerned about her, he'd hardly noticed his own discomfort. He was shaking from cold and exhaustion and he knew they would warm up quicker if they shared their body heat. She didn't protest when he slipped in next to her. She immediately moved closer, seeking his warmth.

Soon Victoria stopped shaking. She murmured something about his having saved her before she dozed off. Jarred was utterly exhausted. Never had he been so close to death. As his body slowly warmed, his muscles began to relax and feeling returned to his numb skin.

He became aware of her lithe body against him. Her fragrance filled his lungs. Her head was on his chest and she was sound asleep. It had been forever since he'd held a naked girl in his arms. He had thought about it often enough, dreamed about Tracey and other girls he'd known. Holding Victoria brought back the sheer bliss of the sensation.

Over the past few days he'd fantasized about holding Victoria, about making love to her. He knew she didn't want him. Why would she? In her eyes he was a mountain man, practically an animal. And yet he'd felt a connection with her—a connection that had grown each day.

She'd said she didn't want him to kiss her. That wasn't the way she'd acted, though. Maybe she didn't know what she wanted. Or maybe she was just afraid of him, afraid of what he might do. That saddened him because he'd done his best to be kind, even though she had done some things to make him angry. And for a long time he wasn't sure what he wanted himself, or even if he could trust her.

Since their dinner the night before, he'd known exactly what he wanted—he wanted her.

Jarred pressed his face into her hair, inhaling her feminine scent, feeling the stirrings of arousal, despite his exhaustion. She was so compliant, lying naked in his arms, so vulnerable. The real question was how would she be later on, when she awoke and had regained her strength? How would she be, once she realized that they were once again alone in the cave?

10

IT MIGHT HAVE BEEN the crackle of the burning wood in the fire pit that awakened her, or maybe it was the sonorous purr of his breathing. Victoria was lying with her arm across Jarred's matted chest, her cheek against the downy softness of his beard. Her leg was wrapped around his muscular thigh, her breast pressing against his side.

In the daze of semisleep, it felt comfortable and natural. As her mind came into focus, the reality of it came as a shock. My God, she was in bed with Jarred, and they were nude!

She disengaged herself as best she could. She looked around to see if there was something she could put on. Nothing. Her scattered clothes were wet rags on the floor of the cave. He had an arm around her and she didn't want to awaken him, so she couldn't move farther away from him.

She tried to recall what had happened. She was able to summon up only the vaguest memories of him undressing her and later slipping under the covers.

Their nakedness, and the implied intimacy, was strangely compelling and frightening.

They were in bed together because of the instinct to survive—a man and a woman who had done what it took to avoid death. But now that they were out of danger, the same old questions came to mind as before.

Jarred—the raw, bearish, physical creature that he was—remained as much a sexual threat as ever. What they'd been through together, the risks he'd taken, the sacrifices he'd made, had softened her heart toward him.

Should she go with her instincts? She'd had her passions, but they hadn't been sexual. When it came to relationships, she had been more controlled than spontaneous, more studied than instinctual.

However, lying naked beside Jarred was firing desires that she had long repressed. Besides, she liked Jarred Wilde. Ironically he was proving to be one of the more caring and tender men she had ever known. A wild man with a gentle heart.

With a blizzard raging outside, she snuggled closer to him again, receiving the warmth of his body with pleasure. The distance between life and death was indeed narrow. If it hadn't been for Jarred, she would have ended up a corpse covered with snow.

Her face felt raw and burned from exposure to the icy wind. She was sore and bruised from falling and being dragged over the hard ground. Her fingers and toes were still a little numb. Still, she was alive, and more aware of her body than she'd ever been before.

She imagined making love with Jarred, submitting to his strength. Despite the fatigue of her muscles, the bruises, the aches and pains, her body began to tingle.

She judged it must be very early morning. The fire had burned low, though Jarred may well have added wood during the night. For a while she watched the shadows dancing on his face, her eye tracing the line of his forehead and nose, his sensuous lips.

She reached out and lightly touched his beard, remembering the feel of it enveloping her face as they'd kissed the other night. Something about it fascinated her. There were enough bearded faces in Berkeley that it was certainly not a novelty to her, and yet, on Jarred it seemed different. There was added significance—a basic, wild elemental quality about it.

He had a wonderfully broad chest, only partially covered at the moment by the bedding. Tentatively she put her hand on it, not wanting to awaken him, yet craving the sensation of the hair against her palm.

She stroked his chest lightly, taking pleasure in the feel of him, aware of the effect it was having on her. When had she ever been so turned on by a man's body? Never. This was so different from any other intimacy she'd known.

It helped that he was sleeping. It gave her an advantage, an opportunity that she wouldn't otherwise have. The tingling and urges within her grew stronger and she felt a certain power. She'd never consciously known such desire, and it intrigued her that she felt it with him.

Unable to resist, she leaned over and kissed his shoulder, again running her fingers through the dense hair on his chest. She put her leg back over his, liking the fiery heat of his skin. Jarred was like an oven—hot and alluring. She wanted to crawl on top of him, she wanted to press against him.

It astounded her how she'd gotten herself worked up. She had to resist the urge to reach for his phallus and take him in her hand. She knew her bravado was only due to the fact that he was asleep. She had to be careful not to wake him. And yet the desire to rub herself against him was so strong, she almost wanted him to know.

When she kissed his arm, Jarred stirred, moaning in his sleep. Victoria tensed, her courage suddenly abandoning her. He shifted slightly, moving his hip against her. Then he seemed to settle back into sleep.

Despite her wonderful fantasies about him, the prospect of him awakening made her nervous. She continued to watch his face until she was sure he wouldn't wake up. Then, sighing, she laid her head down and stared at the ceiling, trying to settle her throbbing body.

Victoria wasn't sure she really wanted to face him in her present state of nakedness. Once more she considered slipping from the bed to go look for something to put on. Better she was clothed when he finally awoke.

She carefully started inching away, her eyes on his face, her heart beating at a steady pace. She lifted the blanket to slip out of the bed when his eyes flickered open. He blinked a couple of times, then turned his head toward her.

"You're awake," he said.

She clutched the blanket to her chest. "Yes."

"How do you feel?"

"I'm okay. How do you feel?"

Jarred smiled. "A lot better than last night."

"We nearly died, didn't we?"

He reached out and put his hand against the side of her face, cupping it affectionately. "Yeah, I would say so."

"It was all my fault. Do you hate me for it?"

He shook his head. "No, I don't hate you."

His kindness was evident once more. As she watched his eyes, she saw he was becoming aware of just where they were. He looked at her mouth and into her eyes before putting his hand on her bare shoulder.

"You're beautiful, Victoria," he said. "I like to look at you."

She swallowed hard, her heart skipping a beat. "I like to look at you, too," she admitted. She didn't know why she'd said it. Maybe the truth couldn't be hidden any longer—she felt a deep aching desire for Jarred.

A curious look came over his face. "Aren't you afraid of me anymore?"

"Yes, I'm afraid of you."

"Then why did you say you like to look at me?"

"I guess because it's true."

Jarred brushed her cheek with the tips of his fingers, then he ran them down the side of her neck and over her shoulder. He kept looking into her eyes, to observe her reaction.

He stroked her hair, as though intrigued by what was happening. Her compliance was not lost on him, and the implied message was as unambiguous as it could be.

He touched her lip with the tip of his finger. Then he ran it down her forehead and along the ridge of her nose. She closed her eyes, her breath coming quicker, and she felt herself moisten.

"Do you like it when I touch you?" he asked, his voice low and resonant.

"Yes," she whispered.

He continued to stroke her head, moving his hand ever so slowly. His thumb traced the line of her jaw like a sculptor examining his work, testing the velvety finish of the stone.

"I want to look at your body," he murmured and, without waiting for her to reply, he folded back the blanket so that she was exposed from the waist up.

He raised himself to his elbow. She looked up into his eyes, seeing them turn dark with desire. Then he trailed his finger across her chest, seeking out first one nub, then the other. Her breasts began to tingle and Victoria moaned softly, closing her eyes. She was startled when she felt his lips close around one of her nipples. It hardened and grew large as he drew his tongue across the tip. Then he leaned over, directly above her face.

"Oh, Jarred," she said, as he slipped his hand behind her neck and covered her mouth. She parted her lips and he slipped his tongue inside. Victoria's heart was beating so hard it ached. She groaned, taking his head and crushing his mouth still harder against hers.

After a while he sat upright, taking her with him, their mouths never parting. He held her cradled in his arms, as she sat in his lap. She felt so small, so overwhelmed by his size and strength.

Jarred was deeply aroused. He ran his hand down her back and over her hip, grabbing her buttocks, sinking his fingers into her flesh.

He lay back then, and pulled her on top of him. Her swollen breasts pressed against him. She could feel his phallus pressing against her. He took her head in his hands and kissed her hard.

She pressed her face in the soft down of his beard as his hands explored her. Then he rolled over so that she was under him and wedged his legs between hers. Her cleft became a river.

Jarred drove into her with a single stroke. She gasped at the sensation, the size of him. And even before he moved, her core pulsed as her excitement began to build.

She dug her nails into his shoulders. "Oh, please," she begged. "Take me. Do it now. Oh, please."

Those words were all it took. He began driving into her, groans of pleasure welling from his throat as his pace quickened. His excitement carried her along and she soon lost all control. Her body started undulating, rippling under him, her legs opened wider as surges of pleasure coursed through her with each thrust.

When she felt herself coming, she grabbed the bear-skin with her fists, lifted her chin for air and cried out. They heaved against each other for several more moments. When it was finally over and she gasped for air, Jarred loosened his grip on her and eased his weight off her body.

"Oh...oh," she moaned. No other words came. She could only groan.

Jarred looked into her half-closed eyes, then kissed her neck, his breath spilling over her sweat-soaked skin. He growled with pleasure.

"God," he said, his chest heaving. "God, Victoria."

They lay still for a long time, managing to do little more than breathe. When her heart finally quieted, Victoria ran her fingers through his tangled hair and kissed his shoulder. He was still inside of her and she liked the feeling, the oneness, the unity. This was sex like she'd never known before.

It had to be special for Jarred, too—if for no other reason than because it had been so long. Only then did the reality of that strike her. Fifteen years of waiting, of deprivation, building to this one perfect moment of release.

She rubbed his back and cuddled him. "Was it good?" she whispered.

"I can't even tell you," he said. There was awe in his voice, marvel. He came out of her and rolled onto his back. He lay still, taking deep breaths.

She glanced over at him. He looked spent, exhausted. He felt for her hand and held it, their fingers entwining. It was a tender gesture, and she appreciated it. It was too early to think about what had happened, what it might have meant, so she just lay there beside him, waiting to come back to earth.

Jarred pulled her hand to his mouth and kissed her fingers. "I didn't hurt you, did I?"

"No, it felt wonderful. I've never made love that way."

"What other way is there?"

She couldn't help laughing. His comment sounded so innocent, so sweet. Yet, she understood exactly what he meant.

"What's so funny?" he asked, sounding slightly annoyed.

"I'm sorry. All I meant to say was it's never been that good before."

"Couldn't Randall make love?" There was a hint of superiority in his voice.

"Not like that."

He rolled his head toward her, a smile playing on his lips. "I guess it wouldn't be much of a compliment to say you're the best I've had in a long time."

She chuckled. "No, it wouldn't be much of a compliment at all." She snuggled closer to him, putting her head on his shoulder as her fingers played with the tangled mat on his chest. "I hope this wasn't a terrible mistake," she said.

"Why? Do you think you might have gotten pregnant?"

"No, that wasn't what I was thinking, though I do have to be very careful."

"What did you mean then?"

"I meant...well...don't you understand, Jarred? It's because of this that I tried to go away. I was afraid this would happen."

"I think you've got it backward, Victoria. This would be a reason to stay, not run away."

He didn't understand and she wasn't going to try to explain. She was still enjoying the intimacy, the pleasure of the moment. She felt so complete.

She ran her hand down over his flat stomach. The muscles were taut and hard. With the first light of dawn coming in the window, she was able to see his phallus rising from the dark tangle of his loins. He was semierect. Even then, he seemed prodigious. She moved her hand away and kissed his chest.

"Tracey thought she was pregnant once," he said, as he stared thoughtfully at the ceiling.

"Did that upset you?"

"It upset her. I guess I was worried, too. I thought we would have to get married."

"Didn't you want to marry her?"

"Her parents didn't think it was a good idea."

"What about you?"

"I thought it would be better if we went to college first. We were arguing about what to do when she found out she wasn't pregnant after all."

"You must have been glad about that."

"It sort of messed things up anyway. Her parents were really upset."

"Whatever happened to her, do you know?"

"A few years after I took off, I asked Macky to find out. He told me she was living in Tacoma. Then later I heard she was married and had a couple of kids. I never asked about her after that."

"Poor Jarred."

"It didn't matter. When I left the world behind, I left Tracey, too. I knew I'd never see her again."

"I'm still having trouble figuring out why you've stayed away so long," she said. "Didn't you realize at some point that you could go back if you wanted to?"

"But I didn't want to."

"Why?"

"Victoria, I don't want to talk about this anymore. Please don't ask me about it."

She put her hand on his shoulder. "I'm sorry. I didn't mean to pry. It's just that I care about you, Jarred."

"Do you?"

"That's why I came in the first place."

"You didn't know we'd make love."

"No," she said. "That's true."

He caressed her face. "Are you glad you're here?"

"Right now, at this moment, I feel very happy."

"That doesn't answer my question."

She looked into his eyes as her anxiety grew. "Why can't anything be easy?"

"In other words, the answer is no."

"In other words, I haven't had time to think about it. My feelings about what I want are very confused."

"Mine aren't," Jarred said.

"No, I don't imagine they are."

"It takes a while," he said, obviously trying to reassure her. "I had difficulty adjusting at first, too."

Victoria looked at him. In his mind she was already his companion for life—or at least he had considered the possibility. It was the very thing she had wanted to avoid. From the first, her instincts had told her that once they got close, it would be very hard to part. Now more than ever, she would be fighting herself as well as him.

11

JARRED WATCHED HER scraping the last of her scrambled eggs from her tin plate. Victoria was wearing one of his old T-shirts, the one that was so thin and full of holes that he never wore it anymore. It was all he'd been able to find for her. Everything else was soaking wet.

"These are delicious for powdered eggs," she said, wiping the corner of her mouth. "If I were you, I'd be eating them all the time."

"They wouldn't last. I've had this box since Macky gave it to me last spring. I told him I'd like some more. I hope he remembers."

She looked at him thoughtfully and Jarred stared right back. Since they'd made love, everything seemed completely different. He no longer felt tense and uncomfortable. And he was so very happy. Victoria seemed as if she might be happy, too, except that he could sense that something was bothering her—something hidden way down deep.

While they'd fixed breakfast, he'd taken her into his arms and asked if she was all right. She'd assured him she was, and she'd acted very definite about it. He didn't press the point, assuming she needed a little more time to adjust.

"What are you going to do if your friend, Macky, moves away, or gets sick, or dies?" Victoria asked.

"I guess I won't be eating eggs or reading library books," he said. "I'd just have to do without some of the luxuries."

She shook her head sadly. "Jarred, I don't know how you can stand living on the edge the way you do."

"Your problem, Victoria, is that you think too much about the future," he said. "If you do that all the time, you miss today."

"You worry about the future, too. Look how you have to plan ahead to survive."

"That's different. That's just using common sense. I try to take each day as it comes, to enjoy it for what it has to offer. And today is my best one ever."

The comment made her smile and she reached out and touched his hand. He took her fingers and held them. But the sadness in her eyes lingered, and it disturbed him.

"Are you sure there isn't something wrong?"

She shook her head and glanced away.

"You know, you really look terrific in that shirt," he said, trying to distract her a bit. "It doesn't cover up so much that I have to use my imagination."

She took the blanket that was draped over the back of her chair and pulled it around her shoulders. "This cave is too damned cold to run around scantily clad for very long. We have to do laundry."

"All right. I can string up some lines to hang it on."

"I'll do the wash, then. I would also like a bath. I don't suppose you have a bar of soap."

"I have two bars."

"Will you share?" she asked.

He pretended to think about it. "Would you like some help washing?"

"Me or the clothes?"

"You."

"I thought that's what you meant." She gave him a chiding look. "I don't think you should be jumping to any conclusions just because I made love with you this morning."

"You said you liked it. That seems to me reason enough to be glad."

She laughed. "You know what, Jarred? You're living proof that men are born thinking with their genitals. It isn't learned behavior."

He chuckled.

"That wasn't meant as a compliment. In fact, it's a criticism."

"If knowing what you want is thinking with your genitals," he said, trying not to laugh, "then I'm guilty."

"It's nothing to be proud of."

He gave her a big grin, and they exchanged looks. He liked the way Victoria talked back to him. He had no way of knowing if that's the way women were these days, or if relations between the sexes were a lot different among adults than the way he'd thought they were as a teenager. All he knew for sure was that this woman in particular appealed to him a whole lot. She was not only sexy and pretty, she was smart and caring and she seemed to understand him.

"Well, let's get started," she said. "If I'm going to be here for a while, we'll have to do some housecleaning and get this place shipshape."

They went to work, and before long the cave looked like a Chinese laundry. Jarred strung up lines and Victoria washed out everything he had, including the clothes he'd been wearing. That meant he had to keep a blanket wrapped around him in order to stay comfortably warm. He did manage to store the venison jerky he'd smoked. After he'd finished that job, Victoria told him he might as well sit in his rocking chair because it was awfully difficult for him to get anything accomplished and hold on to his blanket at the same time.

She worked hard and he watched, enjoying the sight of her dressed only in his old T-shirt. Her legs were slender and long, and he was especially aroused by the sight of her erect nipples straining against the thin fabric. And when he thought of the way she'd reacted when he'd caressed her breasts, the memory aroused him.

He didn't say anything more about the way she looked, because she'd already chided about that once. So he just quietly watched until he couldn't stand the teasing any longer. Then he reached out and yanked her onto his lap. He instantly ran his hand up under the shirt and rubbed her hip. Victoria pulled his hand away.

"Even housewives have to take a break now and then," he said as he nuzzled her neck.

"No housewife cracks," she warned.

When she tried to get up, he held her down, kissing her until she accepted his affection.

Once he'd let her up, she finished the laundry and then went to the back of the cave to give herself a sponge bath. Jarred watched her from his chair, finding the sight of her naked terribly arousing. Every movement she made, each gesture, was done with awareness of him. She never looked at him, but she knew.

He loved looking at her. She had a lovely body, with nicely shaped breasts that were full without being too large. The way she held her head and used her hands and moved her body was all woman.

Victoria washed her hair, then dried herself with his only towel. When she was finished, she wrapped a blanket around her body and came to the fire to let her hair dry completely.

Jarred was mesmerized, not just by the sight of her, but by the fact that such a marvelous woman had come into his life. As Victoria fluffed out her hair, he suddenly became conscious that she was acting the way girls did when they suspected someone was watching them. The realization amused him.

He saw her glance at him from time to time. She didn't do anything to signal that she was interested in making love with him again. He desired her again . . . badly. And knowing she was probably aware of what he was thinking, made his desire all the stronger.

"How long do you think the storm will last?" she asked. "Will it ever stop before spring?" She had gone to the window a few times during the day and stared out at the falling snow.

"There'll be a lot more before winter's over."

"Do you ever go outside?"

"Not during a storm. I do go out on nice days to get exercise and air. After a few months you can feel pretty cooped up."

She clutched her blanket under her chin and stared at the fire.

"Does that bother you, Victoria?"

"You said I worry too much about the future," she said, "so I'm trying not to think about it." She looked at him and managed a weak smile. "I'm thinking about today instead."

She looked so sweet to him, so appealing with her hair all fluffy and her face scrubbed, that he joined her on the pallet by the fire. When he kissed her cheek, she leaned against him in a companionable way. Jarred put an arm around her and held her close.

"I wish we'd left here before this storm," she said. "Together, the two of us. I bet we could have made it back if we'd gone right away."

"No, you were much too weak. As it was, we barely made it back here."

"But it would have been downhill the whole way."

"I wouldn't have gone," he said. "I already told you that."

She sighed deeply, and dropped the subject.

That was what was bothering her—she didn't want to be stuck in the cave for the entire winter.

Jarred figured that if they got a few days of good weather, they might be able to make it out. Getting to Macky Bean's place would be a better shot—and far safer for him. In an emergency, that would be the way to go. The simple fact was, he didn't want Victoria to leave. It might be selfish of him, but as long as she didn't hate him, as long as they enjoyed each other, he would keep her there. With luck, she might even grow to like it.

"What do you miss most?" he asked.

"About civilization?"

"Yes."

"Besides the obvious things like running water, plumbing and electricity, I guess I miss my freedom. I feel like a prisoner here."

"You're no more a prisoner than me."

"Maybe you're just used to it, Jarred."

"It's not as hard as you think to be happy," he said.

She turned and looked at him, her long lashes still damp. "You might be right," she said. "Right now I'd settle for something as simple as a comb."

"Some luxuries are easier to provide than others," he said. "I'll be back in just a second." He got up and went into the sleeping chamber where he kept his personal things. Rummaging around in the semidarkness, he found his comb and took it back out to her.

Victoria smiled when she saw it. "Maybe you're right about how easy it is to be happy." She held her hand out for the comb.

"Mind if I do it for you?" he asked.

"Let me get the tangles out first." She carefully worked through the worst of the tangles before she handed the comb back to him.

Jarred sat down behind her and began combing her hair. She seemed so small to him, all wrapped up in the buckskin. He was aware of her slender neck and shoulders. Kneeling above her as he was, he could smell her fresh, clean scent.

Victoria let her blanket slip down her back so that he could comb the ends of her hair more easily. Her bare white shoulders were alluring, and he couldn't resist the impulse to kiss them. She rolled her head against his as he drew his lips up the side of her neck.

"You smell so good," he whispered into her ear. "Maybe I'll go wash, too. You won't run off, will you?"

She laughed. "I wouldn't get very far in the snow like this, would I?"

Jarred went back to the big tub where he kept his water supply. He filled a pan with enough water to get clean. "Before we use any more water for washing, I'm going to have to melt some more snow," he called to her. "Remind me to fill the tub before we go to sleep tonight."

"What do you do for water in the summer?"

"There's a spring about a quarter of a mile from here. I usually bathe in a creek."

After he'd thoroughly washed and dumped the dirty water down the sump hole, he returned to the fire where he stretched out on the bearskin next to Victoria. Her hand was sticking out of her blanket and he took it, playing with her fingers.

"How long do you think it will be before the clothes dry?" she asked.

"With the heat from the fire, they should be fairly dry by morning."

"Good."

"Don't you like sitting around nude?" he asked.

She sat up and gave him a disapproving look.

"Just think how much more unpleasant it would be if we didn't like each other," he said.

She whacked him on the stomach. "Pervert!" He laughed, liking her playfulness.

"It's been years, presumably, since you've been around women," she said. "So how is it your whole ego structure is built around sexual conquest?"

"Are you trying to tell me I'm horny?" he teased.

She went to hit him again. Before she could manage it, Jarred grabbed her arm and pulled her down next to him. She turned her head his way, her eyes betraying both a touch of uncertainty and expectation.

He lifted himself onto his elbow, cautioning himself to be gentle with her. He touched her cheek with his fingertips as he looked into her eyes. "The way I figure it, I've been here around five thousand days, give or take a few," he said. "Do you think making love twice in one day would mess up my average too much?"

Victoria laughed. "There's absolutely nothing abnormal about you, Jarred Wilde. The only thing that separates you from the rest of the men in the world is a shave and a haircut."

He brought his face close to hers, where he could inhale her scent and kiss her if he wanted to. "You're trying to tell me I need to go to the barber. Is that it?"

"Actually, I'm getting used to the caveman look," she teased. "Besides, for all I know, you might be dreadfully ugly without all that hair."

"The question is not how you feel about the caveman look, it's how you feel about the caveman." He kissed her then, his lips lightly pressing against hers.

Victoria silently stared into his eyes, as if she wasn't sure how to respond. She seemed to be waiting for what was to happen next.

Again Jarred had to hold himself in check. He'd been erect for so long that his first impulse was to rip away the blanket and ravish her. He wanted to be in her again, to feel her moving against him, urging him to go harder, faster. He wanted to watch the look on her face when she surrendered to him, and to her own pleasure.

He slipped his hand under the buckskin blanket and pushed it aside. Her eyes shimmered as she watched him draw lazy circles around her breasts.

He rubbed each nipple, making them swell. She moaned, her glistening eyes still riveted to his as he continued to play with her. Then, when he couldn't hold back any longer, when he had to have more of her, he moved past the plane of her stomach to her mound. He lingered there for a long moment, toying with her moist curls, before moving on to her inner thigh. When his finger found her center, she groaned out loud. It was almost a plea.

Jarred swallowed hard. He could feel his heart pounding against the wall of his chest and he yearned for release, to thrust into her. Yet at the same time he wanted to give her pleasure. He wanted that as much as his own fulfillment. He wanted Victoria to want him.

He began stroking her then, and she closed her eyes, her face raised heavenward, her lips parted. Her long lashes lay on her skin, and she looked so beautiful with the shadows from the fire accentuating the plane of her cheekbones, the fullness of her mouth and the delicate line of her jaw. Color had risen in her cheeks, and he could see the side of her throat pulse with every beat of her heart.

He did kiss her then, worshipfully, and Victoria kissed him back. He quickened his stroking and she immediately arched against his hand, signaling her desire for more.

Jarred paused just long enough to draw his fingers down the length of her cleft, letting them sink several times into the hot pool before he resumed caressing her nub.

Victoria's hips began rocking, and she took his wrist and made the pressure harder still. The sight of her as she worked against his hand was so enthralling that he was afraid he would come.

Finally, unable to hold back any longer, he moved over her. She opened her legs and he pressed his phallus against her. He looked into her eyes to see if she was ready, and she wrapped her legs around his waist, opening herself even wider. He took her then, driving into her with a single stroke.

This time his thrusts were slow, measured, deliberate. Victoria strained to get even more of him, but he always held back, just a little, just enough to keep her on the hard edge of desire, just enough to deny her the ultimate fulfillment she craved.

She was writhing under him, moaning her pleasure, begging for more. Still he held back. She would have her pleasure before he took his, even if it killed him.

Suddenly Victoria dug her nails into his back and arched. He thrust once, twice, then a third time, much harder and faster than before. She cried out his name, the sound echoing through the cave, and felt himself shudder with expectation. He'd never felt such excitement, such potent desire.

"Oh, my God," she said breathlessly. "Oh, my God! Don't stop. Please, don't stop."

They could have been his words, because her excitement had become his excitement, her desire his. Jarred's heart pounded furiously, his loins so ready to explode that what control he had was rapidly slipping away. Her fingers dug into his back, inviting him to give her everything he had. His pace quickened and a groan came from his throat with each thrust, each ragged breath.

Victoria's jaw was taut, her teeth clenched, her agony and ecstasy indistinguishable. They crashed hard against each other. Her moan became a plea, her plea a cry, and her cry a scream. The sound of her voice, the desperation, set him off and he exploded inside her.

Breathless, he collapsed on her. He was so drained, so spent, that he couldn't support his own weight.

For a minute or two he lay on top of her, trying to regain himself, to catch his breath. He had no idea sex could be so consuming, that a woman could take a man so completely, so utterly dominate him by her submission.

Victoria also was motionless, except for the rise and fall of her chest. Her arms were lying limply at her side, her legs had slid back down over his hips to the ground. He managed to lift his head so that he could see her.

Hers was the face of an angel. Her eyes were closed. She looked serene and blissful, as though she were in some distant world. Perspiration was running into the hair at her temples. Fine beads of moisture glistened on her upper lip. Her neck and upper chest were scarlet. An occasional moan passed her lips.

Though it took all his strength to hold himself up, he couldn't stop looking at her. The sensation he felt—the warmth in his heart, the closeness, the oneness—were so intense that his chest constricted. Victoria, this woman he'd possessed and who possessed him, was the most wonderful thing that had ever happened to him. His eyes shimmered with emotion, and a tear ran down his cheek.

At that instant she opened her eyes, looking like someone coming back to life. Her lips widened into a smile, a faint one. Another tear ran into his beard.

She reached up and wiped his cheek with her cool fingers. Then she smiled again, as if to say she understood. There was a power in her serenity that amazed him. He was in awe. Humbled.

Jarred lowered his head and pressed his cheek against hers, taking comfort in this closeness. Emotion swirled through him, and yet he could not begin to express what he was feeling. He didn't know if she felt the same, because she, too, remained mute.

He closed his eyes and snuggled against her, liking it that they were still coupled, that they found peace and fulfillment together. She put her arms around him and he wished, even as he knew it was impossible, that they could remain this way for all eternity.

12

THEY SPENT the rest of the day by the fire. At times they would talk, but for long stretches they would just lie in each other's arms or hold hands, saying nothing.

Victoria felt a strange contentment, and nothing mattered apart from being with him. Even in her torpid condition she felt a new vibrancy, a deep sense of being alive and at one with the man beside her.

Jarred did rouse himself long enough to get a bowl of food from the larder, which he brought to the bed for them to share. They fed each other and, for the first time Victoria could ever remember, she had a sense of the universe shriveling to the size of a single room, and the rest of the human race being embodied in a single man.

Their lovemaking had been so intense, so deeply fulfilling, that Victoria felt that both her body and her spirit had been transformed. Things that had been important before no longer seemed to matter. Sensation had become everything.

Jarred didn't talk a lot, but he frequently touched her, communicating his affection. He absently toyed with her hair or her fingers. Occasionally, he would kiss her or swirl his tongue around her nipple. Once he pressed his ear against her chest and lay there for fifteen or twenty minutes. Finally, she asked what he was doing.

"I'm listening to your heart."

"Is it that interesting?"

"Yes," he said. "It's everything."

She shared the sentiment. At that moment, Jarred Wilde meant everything to her, as well.

It grew dark without their noticing. Victoria wondered if that meant they ought to sleep, or if that was something reserved for mere mortals. She gazed at Jarred's face—in the course of a few hours—or was it a millenium?—he'd become her world.

"If you could be anywhere on earth right now," he said without looking at her, "where would you choose to be?"

"Here."

"Really?"

"Yes, really." She ran her fingers through his tangled hair. "You were very persuasive today."

He took her hand and kissed it.

"Can you think of any other place you'd choose to be?" she asked.

"Other than maybe a bakery...no."

She laughed and leaned over to kiss his forehead.

"But I'd want you there with me," he added.

"Ever the diplomat."

"I'm just practical."

"Which reminds me, didn't you say we needed to melt some snow so we'll have water?"

He groaned lazily. "I hate the thought of putting on damp clothes and going outside."

"Will it wait till morning?"

"I should do it now. It takes a while to melt."

"I'll help you."

"No," he said. "You keep the bed warm."

Jarred took a shirt and a pair of pants from the line, slipped them on, then got a bucket and proceeded to fill the large tub at the back of the cave. He made a dozen or more trips, and by the time he sealed the door and returned to the bed, his skin was icy.

"You aren't touching me, Jarred Wilde, until you warm up," she said, pushing him away when he tried to snuggle against her.

"Next time, I'll let you do it," he teased.

"I offered to help."

"Victoria, don't you know that women were made to keep men warm and comfortable?"

"Boy, do you ever have a lot of catching up to do! And I've got news for you, buster. Robinson Crusoe's man Friday was just that—a man!"

"Who just carried the water?" he replied. "You or me?"

"You have a point," she said. "Come to think of it, you might make a very good Friday."

He gave her a big bear hug, making her squeal because he was so cold. It didn't take him long to warm up. Soon they were comfortably holding each other again. He rested his head on her chest and she stroked his hair.

"What time do you suppose it is?" she asked.

"Night."

"Can't you be more specific?"

"Early night."

"I suppose the date is winter," she chided.

"Early winter."

"It must be December by now," she said wistfully, as she caressed his head. "How many days have I been here?"

"Seven days."

"Let's see, that makes it the first week of December. It'll be Christmas before long."

He didn't say anything.

"Have you missed having Christmas?" she asked. "Did you ever think about the rest of the world celebrating while you weren't?"

He grew solemn. "I suppose at first I did. The second or third winter Macky gave me a transistor radio and some batteries. I listened to Christmas music in December. It only made me feel more lonely and depressed. In frustration I finally threw the thing off a cliff."

The comment brought back the reality of his situation. After experiencing such deep contentment, Victoria didn't want to consider the future. Jarred must have sensed her anxiety because he kissed her deeply, then firmly took her jaw in his hand. "Don't think about it," he said.

"It's not easy to hide anything from you, is it?"

"I'm getting used to you, Victoria." He kissed her again.

"I think I like that," she said.

They made love again, though more tenderly than before. Her excitement wasn't any less for it, however. Jarred's touch had become electric and she craved intimacy with him, she yearned for him to take her.

It was the strangest thing. She couldn't get enough of him, nor did he seem to grow tired of her. They became each other's obsession, each other's addiction. They would sleep, then one of them would awaken the other with an intimate touch, or a kiss, and the love-making would begin all over again.

Victoria lost count of how many times they made love that night, but each time was different and exciting. Sometimes they kissed continuously, their mouths melded. Once he mounted her from behind and, as he drove into her, she saw their shadows dancing on the walls of the cave, and watched herself shudder and collapse under the force of her orgasm.

In the morning Victoria awoke to the smell of eggs and coffee. She sat up to discover that Jarred had already taken the laundry down. He had dressed and was hard at work making breakfast.

"Why didn't you wake me?"

"You were sleeping so peacefully, I didn't have the heart."

She rubbed her eyes. Had all that lovemaking truly been real? Without a doubt she had enjoyed the most fabulous sexual experience of her life. Jarred appeared almost buoyant.

"I put some clothes by the fire for you to put on," he said. "They might be a little damp still. Soon enough they'll dry from your body heat."

"I want to bathe before I dress."

"Better eat breakfast first. It's almost ready. Anyway, if you're going to have a bath, I hope you like real cold water. The snow's only half-melted."

"Can't we heat it up?"

"It would take a six-month supply of butane. Wouldn't you rather have some hot meals?"

"What about using the fire?"

"We can if it's important to you, but it'll take some doing."

"It's important," she said, getting to her feet and wrapping her blanket around her.

"All right. I'll take care of it after breakfast."

She stepped into her moccasins and went to the window. The storm that had raged for two days had broken. The wind was as strong as ever, and she could feel its effect whizzing through the cracks in the wall.

"It's stopped snowing," she said with a shiver.

"Not for long. I think there's another storm brewing."

She stared across the snowy valley, appreciating how absolutely isolated they were. Nature was their buffer against the rest of the world. Although some of her wariness remained, she could actually say she was glad to be trapped alone with Jarred.

It was more than just the attraction she felt and the fulfillment he gave her. In the short time they had been around each other, their common struggle had brought them together in spirit, as well as in body.

She glanced back at Jarred, savoring the sight of him. How easily her recollections of their lovemaking aroused her. She felt the warm glow of it even now. Her body fairly tingled at the thought of being with him.

Looking out at the wintry landscape, she mulled over her situation. It might be a long while before she would be returning to civilization. The prospect of a whole winter of nights like the last one was too good to be true—that is, if she ignored certain realities.

Had she in fact killed Steve Parnell? Or had he survived to spread the story of Jarred's survival? Her disappearance would undoubtedly enhance the credibility of Parnell's claims.

She could count on the fact that if Parnell had made it back to town, he would have told a story that would put him in a good light, and Jarred in a bad one. And if so, everyone would be in an uproar. The tale might even have spread farther than Edgar by now. The national news networks might have picked up on it. If so, come spring, reporters from all over would be swarming into the mountains.

And what would be the impact of her disappearance? With Randall McPherson out of her life, there would be no one devastated by her disappearance. Dr. Walther would be concerned, especially knowing he'd played a part in her adventure, though he couldn't blame himself for what had happened. She was scheduled to teach two classes in the spring semester, and the anthropology department would have to find a last-minute replacement. With no one paying the rent, her landlady would eventually move her things out of the apartment and put them in storage.

All that seemed so abstract and remote that it was hard to know what was real anymore. Was this time with Jarred just an interlude in fantasyland, or did it mean more than that? In April she was due to renegotiate the lease on the ranch. Was it unrealistic to think about that, when she didn't even know what would be happening as soon as Christmas? How could a person who was in hiding possibly plan his or her life?

"Do you want breakfast," Jarred asked, "or would you prefer to spend the morning dreaming about skiing?" He came up behind her and put his arms around her.

"What makes you think I wasn't fondly recalling last night?"

"Were you?"

"Among other things."

He kissed her neck. "Good. I'd feel terrible if you'd already forgotten."

They went to the table. "You are many things, Jarred, but you are definitely not forgettable."

He grinned with satisfaction. "Unfortunately, though, man cannot live on love alone. After we finish eating, I have some work to do."

"What kind of work?"

"Well, for starters, I have to tan the deerskin. It's rolled up in the storage room, seasoning."

"How does one tan a deerskin?"

"With difficulty. And it happens not to be a very pleasant job."

"In other words, I need to be prepared."

"Exactly."

JARRED WAS RIGHT about the tanning. Victoria watched him scraping the remaining flesh and hair from the skin. The smell was not at all pleasant. He used a smooth rock to pound the oils and part of the animal's innards into the skin, explaining that was what made the buckskin soft. He told her that afterward he would smoke the skin over the fire to cure it.

"This living close to nature has its ups and downs, doesn't it?" she said. "It's sort of two steps forward and one step back."

"What were the two steps forward?"

"Come to think of it," she said blushing, "there may have been more than just two."

"Maybe we can try for a little more progress later," he said with a smile.

"Not unless you take a bath first. That animal skin smells to high heaven. Speaking of which, I'd like to get cleaned up myself."

Jarred fixed the fire so she could heat some water. He moved some large rocks into the fire pit to support a pan. He also carried more wood from the storage room. Victoria took care of the rest while he returned to his task.

She heated a couple of gallons of water and poured it into a large tub from the storeroom. By mixing it with cold water from the storage tub, she was able to make herself a nice warm bath. Jarred wandered back while she was bathing.

"I'll be glad to heat you some water," she told him, "but you aren't going to touch me with those hands until you've gotten that smell off you."

She'd dressed in her hand-me-down shirt and pants, combed her hair and had Jarred's bathwater ready by the time he had the skin draped over the smoking oven to dry. While he bathed in the back of the cave, she put on his coat and hat and went outside to collect some snow to replenish the water they'd used. She was more than grateful for a chance to get some fresh air.

She noticed that the wind had picked up. Jarred was probably right about another storm front coming in. That meant it would be impossible to leave. Day by day, they were becoming imprisoned. With an anxious glance at the sky, she went back inside.

Jarred was drying himself as she dumped the last bucketful of snow into the tub.

"How's the weather?"

"It's threatening."

"I guess we'll just have to batten down the hatches and stay as comfortable as we can," he said with a grin.

She put down the bucket and regarded him as he stood before her. His body was familiar to her now, and she knew the way it felt and smelled and tasted. She was easily aroused just looking at him, yet worrying had made her edgy and she wasn't in a mood for intimacy. He reached out, took her hand and drew her to him.

"Jarred, don't you think it's a mistake to use sex to hide from reality?"

"Is that what you think we do?"

She put her head on his chest. "I don't know what I think."

He took her hat off and tossed it aside, running his fingers through her hair. "What's upsetting you?"

"I don't know, I guess I've been going over things."

"Like what?"

"Jarred, do you realize we don't know if Steve Parnell is alive or dead. We don't know if they're looking for you as well as for me. We don't know what's going to happen to us. We don't even know what we're going to be doing for Christmas."

He was silent for a moment before answering, as if he needed time to choose his words carefully. "How would you like it if we got a tree? I can find one. We can make some ornaments and have everything but the lights."

She appreciated his attempt to deflect her concern. "But what about the rest of it?"

"What do you mean—presents and carols and Santa Claus?"

"No, silly, I mean the rest of what I said."

"Let's worry about Christmas first," he said, "and everything else later."

He was trying to keep things light. She supposed that course of action was reasonable considering there was nothing they could do about what was happening in Edgar, and no way of finding out the answers to any of her questions. But somehow that did not assuage her frustration.

"I appreciate what you're trying to say, Jarred. Really, how can you be so cool and collected in the middle of a crisis?"

He rubbed her back. "Is this a crisis?"

"Well, what would you call it? This is not summer camp, you know. I feel really on edge because I don't know what's going to happen to us."

He took her face in his hands and looked into her eyes. "Let's have some nice beef stew for dinner and try not to think about what's going on out there. We'll just do the best we can to be happy."

"That's avoiding the problem. Don't you see? When things get difficult, you can't always run away. You did that when you were eighteen, but you're an adult now.

A point comes when you have to face up to what's happening in your life!"

He lowered his eyes and Victoria saw that she'd hurt him. "I'm sorry," she said. "I didn't mean to be so insensitive. I shouldn't be taking it out on you."

"Taking what out? I don't understand."

She took the towel from his hand and wiped his chest and his shoulder. "Oh, I don't know why I said anything. I guess it's just frustration." She kissed him on the chin. "You're going to catch cold standing around naked. Get dressed and I'll help make dinner when you're ready."

"Yes, Mother."

He laughed and she whacked him one. The she sat in the rocking chair while he dressed.

When Jarred had finished, he came and sat crosslegged at her feet. "The best thing to do is to keep busy," he said. "I was thinking I would make you a winter coat so that we can both go outside when the weather's good. You can help. We'll start in the morning. And whenever you feel restless or bored, you can read one of my books. God knows, there's enough back there to last the winter."

Victoria leaned forward and took his hands. "You want to hear something funny? I came to Washington presuming I was going to tame the Edgar wild man. I was going to observe you and find out how isolation had affected you. And if I was real lucky, I thought I might even talk you into going back to civilization with me. You know what? I'm the one who's changed. It's my eyes that are being opened."

He pulled her down onto his lap and held her tight. "I don't know what being here has done for you. What *you've* taught me is that there's a lot to be gained by sharing my life."

She rested her head on his shoulder and sighed. "You're such a good man," she said. "And such a wonderful lover. It doesn't seem right that we should have to live this way—like at any moment things will crumble down on our heads."

"You feel that way?"

"I feel as if I'm standing at the bottom of a mountain and if I so much as sneeze, an avalanche is going to come crashing down and bury me."

"The snow of winter is the stream of spring."

"Thoreau?"

"No, Bob Simmons, my basketball coach."

She chuckled. "Is he the one who gave you all your wisdom, Jarred?"

"No, I got it all these years I've been waiting."

"Waiting for what?"

"For you."

13

IT SNOWED all night and all the next day. Victoria felt increasingly claustrophobic. Jarred distracted her by asking her to help him make a coat. He'd made three for himself over the years, he told her. Once Macky had given him a bright blue parka, but it was too dangerous to wear outside in the daylight because he could be easily spotted. So, he'd come to prefer his own homemade buckskin.

They worked all day into the night, cutting, sewing and fitting the coat to size. Jarred lined the buckskin with rabbit fur, using the last of the pelts he had in storage. He got up early the next morning to finish the sleeves and collar so that the coat was ready for her when she awoke. Smiling proudly, he presented it to her.

Victoria slipped it on. It was warm and it fit her quite well. Although the seams were crudely sewn and it was fastened with ties rather than buttons or a zipper, she loved it, as much because it was made by him as for any other reason.

With the coat snugly around her, Victoria went to the window to check the weather. She was barely able to glimpse the clear, blue sky because snowdrifts covered half the windowpane. "Thank God the sky's not overcast," she said. "If it snows much more, we'll be buried."

"I think we should go out for a walk after we eat," Jarred said. "Might as well give the coat a test."

They literally had to dig their way out. The sunshine felt good, and once they got beyond the entrance to the cave, it was much easier to walk. The snow wasn't nearly as deep on the ridge line above them, so they strolled there, inhaling the biting air and enjoying the vista.

There was a vantage point that afforded a limitless view of the valley below and the snowcapped mountains. For a long time they stared at the view, awed by the beauty of nature.

Victoria pressed her face against his shoulder to shelter it from the wind, and Jarred put his arm protectively around her. She felt so close to him, so happy. He was indeed a very special man.

Lovemaking with them had practically become a way of life. Even when they'd worked on her coat the day before, they'd taken a break and ended up making love amid the scraps of leather and fur. Jarred had held her head in his hands, and looked straight into her eyes as he came, murmuring her name.

That time especially, she'd sensed his love. Each time they were together it was more and more evident how strong their feelings for each other had become.

Their developing relationship was a source of joy, and a cause for anguish. In a matter of days she would be entering her fertile period. She would have to make it clear that they couldn't make love for several days in the middle of her cycle.

She'd always been regular and had never had a pregnancy scare, but even with abstinence they would be taking a big risk. The bottom line was, the life they were leading was like a time bomb. Victoria couldn't allow her growing love for Jarred muddle her thinking.

"So how's the coat?" he asked. "Think it will do?"

"It's the best coat I've ever had."

He beamed with satisfaction. She reached up and kissed him.

"Shall we walk a little more?" he asked.

"I want to ask you a question first," she said.

Jarred read the anxiety in her voice. "What? What's the matter?"

She bit her lip. "The last several days have been some of the most wonderful of my life," she began. "Being with you has been truly extraordinary."

"For me, too."

"I know you care about me," she said.

"So what's the problem?"

"The problem is, we've been deceiving ourselves. This can't go on. It can't last. Not this way."

"Why not?"

"Jarred, I can't stay here forever. It's not practical. It's a fantasy that we're living."

He grew silent.

"Don't you understand that?" she asked.

"I've been here a long time," he said. "And I'm happy."

"Yes, but . . . I'm not like you. My life has been very different from yours."

He wasn't responding. He wouldn't even look at her. It suddenly seemed hopeless to her. How could she reach him? And what did he expect—that she would become a cave dweller, too, living as his mate?

"Tell me what your plans are," she said, taking his hand. "Tell me what you see us doing in the future."

He turned his deep blue eyes on her, staring at her with compelling intensity. She waited. Finally, he said, "I love you, Victoria. I want this to go on forever."

His words were dear to her. And though he was rugged and manly, at that moment he seemed to possess the innocence of a boy. She could imagine him uttering the same sort of thing to his high school sweetheart, Tracey. And suffering then, just as he was suffering now.

Her eyes filled and she reached up and pulled his head down so she could kiss him. Their lips touched. Jarred had been hurt, and he'd withdrawn. "Don't be upset with me," she pleaded.

"What is it *you* want?" he asked. "What are *your* plans?"

"I want us to be together, but not here."

He shook his head. "No."

"I know you said you don't want to go back, that there's nothing for you in Edgar. That isn't what I'm suggesting. You can come with me to California. In the spring, the lease on my ranch is up. It wouldn't be like living in a city, or even a town. There's nature all around just like this, Jarred. You could learn to adjust there. And I could help you."

He stared off at the snowy peaks again. "I can't."

"Why not? Because you're afraid?"

He shook his head. "No, that's not it."

"Then what?"

He wouldn't answer.

"Jarred, talk to me. Don't you see you can't run from this problem forever? What happened to you, happened years ago. You can't let something like that ruin your entire life!"

"You don't understand," he said.

"No, of course I don't understand. Because you won't tell me what the problem is!"

He turned to face her again, his expression as sad as any she'd ever seen. He started to speak, then stopped, his voice breaking. "Todd Parnell didn't die by accident."

She felt the blood drain from her face. "What do you mean? What are you saying?"

"I wanted to kill him. He died because I wanted him to die."

She was shocked. They were the last words she would have expected from his mouth. "Are you trying to tell me you did it on purpose?"

"In a way, yes. I was angry. Todd had been harassing me for a long time, mainly because of Tracey. That night he tried to pick a fight. He said some terrible things to Tracey, just to make me mad. I couldn't take it anymore. I blew my top. We started fighting and something sort of snapped inside of me. I couldn't stop hitting him. Not until I knew he was dead."

"But Tracey said you fought in self-defense. She said you were only defending yourself."

"At first that was true. Then I lost control. I didn't stop hitting him when I should have."

"That doesn't make you a murderer. The law takes the circumstances into consideration. The prosecutor decided against bringing charges."

"Tracey lied for me. I knew she would. I made my decision to go away. I knew I'd never return."

"But that was years ago, Jarred."

He took her by the shoulders, his eyes bleary with tears. "I know what I did, and I've had to live with it. That's why I'm here, Victoria. Nothing can ever change what's happened. This is where I belong."

"If you made a mistake, you've already paid for it."

"My first life ended when I left Edgar," he replied. "It's gone forever. This one is the only one left."

"But things are different now. You aren't alone anymore," she insisted.

"That's true only so long as you stay."

She was on the verge of crying. Jarred's life now seemed doubly tragic.

Victoria had no words of reassurance to offer him. All she could do was put her arms around him and hold him. She was beginning to see that things were completely beyond her control. And with a heavy heart, she acknowledged that when she left, she would be losing him forever.

JARRED'S REVELATION had an immediate effect on their relationship. Victoria had no doubt that he had vilified himself far more than was warranted. The punishment he had meted out was self-imposed exile. No wonder he had suffered such strong feelings of alienation.

In the days following, Victoria tried to discuss the issue, but Jarred refused. The only thing that mattered, he said, was whether or not she intended to stay with him.

Their impasse was compounded by her concern about getting pregnant. When she explained that she would have to abstain during the middle of her cycle, Jarred said he understood. The end result was to amplify the strain developing between them.

For over a week, they lived under a cloud. On the surface they were polite and friendly to each other, but the closeness and warmth they'd shared seemed at an end. Jarred remained considerate and thoughtful, yet distant. Victoria hated what was happening to them.

The first night he said he would return to the sleeping chamber, but Victoria had insisted that he stay with her. He complied, even holding her during the night, but by the third day he said it was just too hard to sleep with her given the fact that they could no longer make love.

She decided he didn't intend his aloofness as punishment because he would show her affection, and they did often kiss, but there was hurt in his eyes whenever she withdrew. And regret. She was at least thankful that Jarred didn't pressure her in any way.

Since the weather was unsettled, they mostly stayed indoors. Jarred had a lot of chores to do and he made the items he needed. Victoria cleaned and organized things for him, did some mending and they both spent long hours reading.

Once, around the middle of the month, there was a relatively clear day. Since they both had cabin fever, they decided to go for a long walk. The air was cold but being outside lifted Victoria's spirits. Jarred seemed a little happier, too, and she was grateful for that.

Having gained the top of the ridge where the wind kept the snow packed to a minimum, Victoria began running, craving the exercise and the exhilaration of the wintry air. Looking back after she'd gone a ways, she waved for Jarred to follow, calling that she would race him to the outcropping of rocks that was a hundred yards or so along the ridge.

He took off after her. Soon the race became a chase. Jarred shouted that when he caught her she was going to get her face washed with snow. She screamed with glee, and threatened him with death if he did. She'd had a thirty-yard head start, and ran at top speed, slipping and sliding over the icy ground.

When they were twenty yards from the rocks, Jarred caught her, grabbing her by the waist and throwing her into a snowbank. He pounced on top of her and pushed her face down into the snow.

"You bastard!" she shouted, as she came up sputtering. Jarred laughed as she sat buried to her waist, spitting out snow and wiping the powdery stuff from her eyes and hair. "Wait till I get you!"

"And what would a one-hundred-and-ten-pound weakling like you do if you could catch me?" he said, rolling away, just beyond her reach.

"Oh!" she said, pointing an accusing finger. "You're no better than the chauvinistic cowboys back home who used to say I couldn't be in the rodeo because I was a girl."

"Were they wrong?"

"Yes, wise guy. And so are you!"

Victoria had scooped up a handful of snow behind her back and lunged at him. She'd caught him off guard and managed to get most of the snow in his face, turning his beard white as flour. Now Jarred was the one sputtering. She squealed with delight, then pounced on top of him, knocking him onto his back. She stuck her face right in his.

"Don't you ever call me a weakling again, Mr. Wilde, or you'll get a lot worse than that!"

"It was a mistake not to finish you off when I had the chance," he said. "I guess I'm just too softhearted."

"Your Mr.-Nice-Guy routine is all an act," she said, her voice modulating as a sudden awareness overcame her. "I know you're really wild at heart."

Their faces were only inches apart, their steamy breaths mingling as they looked into each other's eyes. It had been a while since they had kissed, and she felt a sudden and strong desire for him. She lowered her mouth to his and their lips brushed tenderly.

The hunger that had been building during their period of abstinence flared, and they began kissing more eagerly. Victoria suddenly felt she couldn't get enough of him. She gingerly bit his lips.

They were kissing so passionately that she was startled when Jarred suddenly wrenched his mouth away. She blinked as she saw the alarm on his face.

"What's the matter?"

"Shh!"

He was listening. Then she heard it—the sound of an aircraft engine. Her first thought was that it was a helicopter. No, the sound was different. She rolled off of him and as she started to get up, Jarred held her still.

"Don't move," he said.

Victoria looked up and saw the aircraft. It was more than a thousand feet above them and was banking almost directly overhead. "Shouldn't we hide?"

"Out in the open like this, we're easy to spot," he said. "But it's motion that attracts the eye. Our only chance is to be perfectly still."

"What would happen if they saw us?"

"I suppose it depends on who it is up there. Any pilot who knows this area could radio in a sighting. And the authorities know that no one would be up here this time of year unless there was something wrong."

"Or it was us," she added.

"Yes, unless it was us."

The airplane flew off. There was no indication whether it had sighted them or not.

"What do you think?" she asked.

"My guess is we weren't spotted. You never know. If I'd been paying closer attention, and heard it sooner, we'd have had time to hide in the rocks."

"It's my fault."

"No, the problem is I'm too damned attracted to you," he said.

Victoria lay back on top of him. She gave him a peck on the lips. "I'm too damned attracted to you, too."

"We've got a real problem, don't we?"

She shook her head.

"What do you mean, no?"

"I think I'm safe again, so we really don't have a problem at all."

"Are you suggesting something, Victoria?"

"In a word, yes."

JARRED HAD BUILT the fire to a roaring blaze to really warm the cave. They'd made love frantically, unable to get enough of each other. Twenty minutes after they'd finished the first time, they started in again. They were both soaked with perspiration when they came, and Victoria felt totally and exquisitely spent.

After Jarred had gotten off of her, she lay on her back, exhausted, her legs parted, her arms limp at her sides. Faint pulses were still rippling in her belly, an attenuation of her orgasm. Even her fingers and toes were tingling.

Jarred, too, was lingering in his pleasure. She could tell by his breathing that he was in the same state as she. They weren't touching, but they were as close in spirit as two people could be.

"Is it always like this for you?" he asked.

"You mean with other men?"

"Yes."

"God, no."

"Why not?"

"You're talented, Jarred."

Being a man, he liked having his ego stroked, but Victoria was willing to give him the satisfaction of a compliment. He had, she decided, earned it.

After a few minutes he got to his elbow, leaned over and lightly kissed her lips. Then he got to his feet and wandered over to the window. Victoria watched him staring out at the sky. Somehow she knew he was worrying about the airplane.

THEY MADE LOVE AGAIN after they went to bed, this time more slowly and tenderly than before. For a long time they held each other in silence and Victoria fell asleep that way, in his arms.

The day set the tone for the rest of the week. The warmth and closeness between them had returned, but it wasn't quite the same as before, because they knew they were living on borrowed time.

One evening after they'd heated a tub of water, they bathed each other and made love tenderly under the buckskin blanket. Victoria lay with her head on his shoulder, talking about her grandmother and the ranch.

Jarred listened to her tale, then said, "I've lost track, but isn't it supposed to be Christmas pretty soon?"

"In a couple of days."

"You've been counting."

"I love Christmas," she said.

"Why didn't you say something? We talked about having a tree and decorating it."

"Do you really want to? I thought you were just being polite."

"I'm only sorry we can't have presents and wrapping paper and all that."

"What would you give me, if you could go to any store and afford to buy anything you found?" she asked.

He thought for a moment. "I guess it would be electricity, running water and plumbing. Whatever it took to keep you here."

She nudged him in the ribs. "Men just love practical gifts, don't they?"

"What would you give me?" he asked.

"That's easy. I'd want to give you the power to forgive yourself."

He grew silent.

"What you don't understand," she said, "is that the rest of the world has already forgiven you for what happened to Todd Parnell. You have only to forgive yourself."

"I'm not so sure the rest of the world *has* forgiven me," he replied.

"You can't judge everyone by Steve Parnell. He and his brother both had problems. And Steve is just plain antisocial. He is not a good person."

"I think we should talk about Christmas," he said predictably. "It should be a nice day tomorrow. I'll take my ax and go well down below the timberline where the trees aren't so scraggly and I'll find a nice one."

"All right," she said, relenting. "And while you're gone, I'll see what I can find around here to make some ornaments."

The next morning she watched him putting on his coat and mittens and fur hat. When he was ready, she snuggled her way into his arms.

"Be a good girl while I'm gone," he said, tapping the end of her nose with his finger.

"You be careful," she said. "I don't want anything happening to you."

"God, Victoria, you're starting to sound like a mother."

She gave his beard a yank. "I bet at some level it would tickle you pink if I got pregnant."

"I have to do a lot of things without help, living like I do. I don't think delivering a baby is one I want to try."

"Believe me, it's one job you'll never have to worry about."

He swallowed hard. "I know."

Victoria grabbed his hand and pressed it to her breast. "I love you, Jarred Wilde. I want you to know that."

His eyes started glistening as he looked at her. "That's the nicest thing anybody has said to me in fifteen years." Then, kissing her, he took his ax and slipped out the door into the icy wind.

Victoria secured the leather flap with the rock and turned to look at the cave that had been her home for the better part of a month. With Jarred gone, it seemed somehow different to her. She hadn't been alone there more than several minutes since that time he'd gone hunting. Primitive as it was, it had been a place she'd shared with him.

She sat in the rocking chair and gazed at the flickering flames. She tried to look ahead to the future, but it was impossible to see beyond Christmas. Had she fallen prey to Jarred's way of thinking—living day by day and letting the future take care of itself?

She hadn't given much serious thought as to how and when she'd be leaving. The snows and Jarred's love had made staying the easy option. Did that mean she'd resigned herself to being here until spring?

Victoria didn't want to think about that just then. In the back of her mind she was worrying about Jarred, which on the surface seemed kind of silly. He was more than capable of taking care of himself. Anyway, what would she do when she got back to California, knowing Jarred was alone in his cave or wandering about the

Cascades? She would probably think about him incessantly.

She pulled the rocking chair over near the window for better light and tried reading. Unable to concentrate, she scouted around for a mindless task to occupy her. Over the past weeks they'd worked hard, so there really wasn't much left to do.

She wasn't particularly hungry, but she ate an apple anyway. When she'd finished, she put her hands on her hips and said aloud, "Oh, damn!" The simple fact was, she was going stir-crazy.

The solution was to get outside for some air and exercise. After tying a layer of skins around her moccasins and putting on her coat, hat and mittens, Victoria went outside. The chilly air was very still, which was unusual. Sun was breaking through the broken clouds.

She tromped her way through the snow to the ridge line where she normally walked with Jarred. It seemed strange to be there without him. She'd grown so used to his company that alone she felt incomplete. She really did love him, and that was plenty cause for concern.

If her love was for real, how would she ever deal with losing him? She couldn't imagine making trips back to the mountain to visit. With Jarred, it would be all or nothing. It was either live a phantasmagoric life with him, or return to her own world.

Victoria was so wrapped up in her thoughts that she didn't hear the airplane. When the sound of the engine finally broke through her reverie, she saw the plane gliding high over the valley. A stab of horror went

through her. She was in an open area right on top of the
ridge. There was no place to hide within fifty yards.

She froze, remembering what Jarred had said about
movement attracting the observer's eye. She knew,
though, she must stand out as plainly as the Statue of
Liberty in New York Bay. Very slowly, she crouched
down, to make herself as small as possible.

To her dismay, the plane banked and turned toward
the ridge line on her side of the valley. Then, as she
watched, it circled back toward her. Unlike the previous time, it did not fly away. It held to a tight bank, circling overhead like a giant vulture eyeing a carcass on
the snowy ground.

By the third loop, with each time around at a lower
altitude than the last, it was evident she had been spotted. The only question was what the consequences
would be. It terrified her to think that she had compromised Jarred. If this mistake ended up bringing the authorities down on them, he would never forgive her.
And she would never forgive herself.

After an excruciating five minutes, the plane finally
flew off in the direction it had come. Victoria didn't
know what to think, she didn't know what to do. At
least she hadn't been seen coming out of the cave. She
was several hundred yards from it at the moment, and
she knew it was imperative she get out of sight as
quickly as possible.

She ran back to the cave. She was sweating by the
time she pushed her way inside. Her heart was pounding. She had a terrible, sickening feeling. Somehow she
knew that the world she'd left behind had thrust itself

back into her life. The question was whether this new world she'd found with Jarred would be destroyed?

JARRED FIRST HEARD the plane after he'd already worked his way well down the mountain. He'd been careful to avoid the deep snow, where there was always a danger of avalanche, but when he had seen the plane, alarm bells went off and he'd scampered into a thicket of trees.

For several minutes he'd watched the aircraft circling over the ridge not far from the cave. Had the pilot sighted something? Jarred had walked along that section on his way down the mountain and could have left tracks in the snow; he doubted they would have attracted the pilot's attention. There must have been something else he had spotted.

The airplane that had flown over the week before had given him pause, and this one doubled his anxiety. He decided he should return to the cave right after finding Victoria the perfect tree.

Descending another five hundred feet down the escarpment, he came to a stand of pine where he chopped his firewood each fall. Since Victoria had said she wanted one six or seven feet tall, he confined his search to trees of that height. Working his way deeper into the forest, eliminating tree after tree, he finally found the one he wanted. It was only a little bit taller than he, and was perfectly shaped. He could picture Victoria's smiling face when he brought it into the cave.

He began chopping and had the tree down with half a dozen swings of the ax. After trimming off some of the lower branches, he dragged it by the trunk, retracing his steps through the woods.

The last time he'd gotten a Christmas tree had been when his mother had been dying. She had given him five dollars and the key to her car to go pick one up. All he could get for the money was a scraggly little thing that he'd set up in her bedroom so she could see it. He'd decorated it while she watched. She'd died a month later, the morning after their big game with Chehalis.

Jarred had also assumed that it would be the last time he would share Christmas with anyone he deeply cared for. But with Victoria in his life, some of his old feelings about the holidays had been rekindled, and he found himself looking forward to celebrating again.

He started slogging back up the mountain, the tree in tow, when he heard another aircraft engine in the distance. Searching the sky, he finally spotted a helicopter coming up the valley. The airplane had spotted something, and now the chopper was coming to investigate.

The helicopter angled directly toward the ridge above him. To his utter dismay it hovered at about the place where the large open area was on the ridge, then settled toward the ground.

Realizing the craft had landed fairly near his home, panic welled inside him. Had they spotted the cave? He stood there helplessly, peering up the slope, listening as the chopper's engine fell silent.

"Oh, my God," he said aloud, his chest heaving. It had to be a search party. There was no doubt in his mind. Victoria was in danger!

He was a couple of miles from the cave, with over two thousand feet of vertical climb ahead of him. It would take at least an hour to get back. Tossing the tree

aside, he began scampering up the snowy slope, using
his hands as well as his feet. Within minutes, the icy air
was searing his lungs. But it didn't matter; nothing
mattered but getting to Victoria!

14

IT ONLY TOOK THEM fifteen minutes to find her. All they had to do was follow her tracks in the snow. Victoria was sitting in Jarred's rocking chair when the first officer burst through the door, rifle in hand.

"Freeze!" he shouted.

Two other men rushed in behind him, one in a baseball cap with a star on it, the other in a stocking cap. Both had on sheriff's patrol parkas with badges. They also carried rifles.

"Where's Wilde?" the first man shouted.

"Jarred's not here," she said, her voice tremulous. Her entire body was shaking as she stared at the officers, afraid that at any moment she might be shot.

"Check it out, Jim," the man in the Western hat said.

One of the men handed his rifle to the other, took a handgun from his holster and a flashlight from his utility belt, then began searching the cave. He looked in the sleeping chamber and the storage room, emerging from the storage room with Jarred's rifle in his hand.

"It's clean," he said, holstering his weapon.

"Check the woman."

The deputy had Victoria stand up as he searched her for weapons. When he'd finished, he told her to sit down again. Then the first man who'd come in the doorway pushed his hat back off his forehead and stared down at her.

"Are you Miss Ross?"

"Yes," she said.

"I'm afraid I've got to arrest you."

"What for?"

"Assault on Steve Parnell."

She blinked. "He was attempting to *rape* me."

"Well, ma'am, it's not my job to sort all that out. We've been searching for you for weeks now, not sure whether we were looking for a corpse or a fugitive." He glanced around. "I take it this is Wilde's place."

"Yes. He saved my life, literally. I'd have died if it wasn't for him."

The other two men were wandering around the cave. "Lordy," the one named Jim said. "There's provisions here for a year. And look at all this stuff he's got, Rog. The guy's for real. Parnell was telling the truth about him."

"Where is Wilde now, Miss Ross?" the officer in charge asked.

"He left this morning. I don't know when he'll be back. Maybe not for days."

"He could be hidin' out, Rog," one of the officers said.

"Listen," Victoria said, "what happened between Steve Parnell and me has nothing to do with Jarred. There's no reason for you to bother him. He did me a kindness. He brought me here when I was injured and dying. Then, when the snow came, it was impossible for me to leave."

"One of our patrol planes spotted you this morning, Miss Ross. You didn't exactly act like a person desperate to be rescued."

"I'm not. I *am* concerned for Jarred because he's an innocent victim in all this." She got to her feet. "Look, if you intend to arrest me, then let's get on with it. I'm going to bring charges of my own against Steve Parnell. I'd like to get this over with."

"I want to talk to Wilde. According to Parnell, the wild man saw you clobber him. If he's a material witness, we'll want to take him in, too."

"Jarred can't help you. Anyway, he won't come back. Not while you're here."

The officer turned to one of the deputies. "Jim, run back up to the chopper and ask Ben how much ground time we can have."

"I insist on going now," Victoria said.

"Just sit down, miss," the man in the Western hat said. "We'll go when I say we're going."

Victoria sat back down. This intrusion seemed so unjust. Jarred certainly didn't deserve it. And it was all her fault.

She prayed he would stay away until they'd gone. Jarred had never mentioned having other hideouts. Even if he had one, he would still have lost the only home he'd had for fifteen years. And now that they knew he was alive, folks were bound to hound him. Furthermore, if the police didn't come back, the press or others might.

"Damn," the deputy said, holding up a basket Jarred had made. "The guy's a regular caveman. I can't believe it."

"Yeah, but where'd he get the rest of this stuff? Suppose he stole it?"

Rog looked at Victoria. "Did Wilde tell you much, Miss Ross, how he survived for all this time? I mean, the guy's got to be squirrelly."

"I can assure you, he's quite sane. And he's done nothing wrong."

Jim returned after several minutes. "We can stay half an hour," he said. "An hour tops."

Rog took off his hat and scratched his head, then he looked at Victoria.

"Please," she said. "I've been through a very difficult experience. I want to go."

"Jim and me can stay here and wait for him," the deputy said. "You can pick us up in the morning."

"No, don't," Victoria pleaded. "Jarred doesn't deserve this."

Rog squared his hat. "You have a coat you can wear?" he asked her.

She got the coat Jarred had made for her. The officer looked at it. "This Wilde must be quite a guy."

"He is," she said. She looked into his eyes imploringly. "Please, leave him in peace."

He sighed, then finally he gestured to the other two men. "Come on, boys, let's get out of here."

JARRED WAS WITHIN five hundred feet of the ridge when he heard the helicopter's engine spring to life. He couldn't see the aircraft until it lifted above the crest of the mountain, turned and moved off down the valley. He stood watching it, buried to his thighs in snow. He was sweating so heavily he was soaked, his chest heaving. He was too late.

In his gut, he knew Victoria was gone. In another twenty minutes he passed the place where the craft had set down. The footprints were mostly boots, but there was another, smaller pair, and they were moccasins.

As he neared the cave, it occurred to him it might be a trap, that they might be waiting. He paused outside the entrance, calculating the danger. Then he realized he didn't really care anymore. If they'd taken Victoria, nothing else mattered.

The cave was empty. The fire was barely flickering. He called out her name, getting no response. He glanced around, seeing that they had given the place a cursory search. Then he dropped down on the pallet where they'd slept together, where they'd made love. Tears ran down his cheeks.

Jarred pulled off his hat and his coat, but left on his sweat-soaked shirt. Throwing his head back, he let out a mournful wail.

HE WAS UP and dressed before dawn. He ate hastily and was outside as the first light was beginning to show in the east. He made his way over the ridge and started down the back side of the mountain.

Jarred had never undertaken this trip in the dead of winter. He would make it if he had to crawl the entire way. He'd slept and eaten and regained his strength, and that was all he needed. At least he would be going mostly downhill.

All day Jarred walked on the route he'd followed so many times before. On previous occasions he'd lugged a table, the rocking chair, heavy tubs and as much as eighty pounds of supplies up this grade, but never through waist-deep snowdrifts, and never in freezing temperatures.

In a few hours he'd made it down the steepest part of the climb, then he entered a forested gorge that broadened into a canyon. The going was very slow. Around midday he stopped to rest by a stream, drinking from the icy water and eating from the pouch of provisions he'd brought.

He had to travel light to make it before dark, so he hadn't brought a blanket. Looking at the sky, he estimated it would be touch and go.

Resuming his trek, he followed the stream through a dense forest, then down another gorge. By the time he arrived at the base of the mountain, it was nearly dusk. The last mile was sheer hell. Finally, as darkness fell, Jarred staggered to within sight of Macky Bean's cabin. He could see a dim light coming from the window. The sight gave him not only a shot of adrenaline, but a feeling of hope.

Macky's four-wheel-drive truck was sitting by the house, buried in snow. His friend hadn't used it in a long time, perhaps weeks. Jarred pounded on the front door. When there was no answer, he pushed the door open. The main room was littered and dirty, as usual. A kerosene lantern was sitting on the table along with an empty whiskey bottle.

"Macky!" he called. "Macky, you here?"

There was no response. There was a small bedroom in back. Jarred took the lamp and made his way there. Macky was sprawled out on the bed, his mouth agape, snoring. Though fully dressed, he was half-covered by the tangled bedding. A booted foot hung down the side of the bed to the floor. Macky was in one of his drunken stupors.

Holding the lantern up, Jarred reached down and shook the old man's shoulder. "Macky," he said. "Wake up!" He shook him again. All he got was a groan. "Macky, it's me, Jarred. I need to borrow your truck."

It was futile. Jarred looked around the stale-smelling room, wondering if he could find the keys on his own. He'd planned to leave for Edgar at once. Perhaps he'd be better off waiting until morning.

Sighing in resignation, he removed Macky's boots, hoisted the old man's leg onto the bed and covered him with the blanket. Then he returned to the front room and dropped into the tattered, rump-sprung recliner. He was exhausted, but he knew he wouldn't be able to sleep because he kept thinking about Victoria. All day long he'd pictured her face, worrying, not knowing exactly what had happened to her.

The decision to go after her had been made almost at once. He didn't have to agonize. It really had been very simple. His life no longer meant anything without her.

When he'd rested awhile, Jarred got up, took off his coat and made a fire. Then he rustled up something to eat. When he'd had his fill, he looked in on Macky again. The grizzled old man hadn't moved.

As Jarred turned to leave the room, he caught a glimpse of himself in the cracked mirror over the chest of drawers. He stared at the wild mane of hair and full beard, knowing that was the image Victoria had seen, the face of the man she'd come to love.

Closing his eyes, he tried to visualize himself as a boy, when he'd last been clean-shaven. He knew he wouldn't resemble that person now, even without a beard. But no matter what he looked like, Jarred decided that if he was to return to Edgar, it would not be as a wild man.

He began rummaging through the top drawer of Macky's chest until he found a pair of scissors. Then, he hacked away at his beard until there was only a quarter to a half inch of stubble left on his jaw. After he'd done that, he cut his hair, trimming it to collar length as best he could.

Macky always shaved with a pan of water and a straight razor. He couldn't find the razor in the drawer. Lifting the lantern, he spotted it in the corner of the room, next to a pan of water with soap scum still in it.

Jarred got everything ready and proceeded to shave. He managed to get off the stubble, only nicking himself a few times. When he was done, he stared at his image.

He didn't recognize the man staring back at him. The clean-shaven guy in the mirror was the man he'd become over the past few weeks—transformed by Victoria's love. Slowly but surely, she'd helped him shed his old skin until he was no longer the person he'd been.

"Victoria," he mumbled, "I sure hope you like me as a regular guy."

Blood oozed from his nicks so he stuck some pieces of tissue on them to make the bleeding stop. Then he swept up the hair from the rough plank floor and put it in the trash. He owed it to Macky to clean up a little, but he was just too tired.

Jarred added a couple of pieces of wood to the fire and plopped into the recliner. No sooner had he closed his eyes than he was fast asleep.

EARLY THE NEXT MORNING Jarred shook Macky Bean awake. The old man stared at him through bleary eyes and blinked a couple of times, his thin wisps of gray hair plastered to his skull, his red nose and cheeks contrasting sharply with his pasty skin. It took Macky a couple of seconds to comprehend what he was seeing.

"What? Who the hell are..." He squinted at him. "Jarred?"

"Yeah, it's me."

"What happened to you?"

"Last night I had a little bout with your razor. I hope you don't mind."

"What are you doing here?" the old man croaked.

"You've got to drive me into town, Macky. It's really important."

Macky shook his head, obviously still in an alcoholic daze. "I can't drive nowhere, son. Haven't been in the truck in three weeks. Don't even know if it will start."

"I have to get to town."

Macky closed his eyes. He was clearly in pain. "Give me a little time, son. I feel like hell."

"Macky..."

The old man's eyes closed and Jarred knew it was useless. He left the room. He considered walking into town, but it would take him all day. Better to give Macky a few more hours of rest.

The old man was still under the weather at nine o'clock. Around ten, Jarred tried again. "Macky," he said, "this is more important than anything you've ever done for me. My whole life depends on it."

Macky opened one eye and studied him. "This really is you, is it, son?"

"It's me, Macky."

"Then go, if you can start the blasted thing. The keys are on a hook inside the pantry." He closed his eyes again.

Jarred patted the old man's shoulder. Then he fetched the keys, put on his coat and went outside. At mid-morning the woods were as still as a church. He swept the snow off the truck and got in the cab. He studied the dash. God, he thought, what do I do first?

He depressed the clutch and turned the key in the ignition. The engine groaned miserably, but wouldn't turn over. After a struggle, it fired, sputtered and slowly came to life.

"Hang on, Victoria!" he shouted. "I'm coming!"

There was a foot of snow on the plowed roadbed. Jarred soon got the hang of driving again. Conditions made it impossible to go fast and at times he virtually stopped to keep from sliding into a ditch. It took the better part of an hour to reach the highway.

The asphalt ribbon bisecting the valley looked so strange to him. The sleek vehicle racing toward him seemed even stranger. Another car came down the road from the opposite direction. Then a truck and a pickup with a camper. Jarred knew he couldn't sit there all day watching the cars, so when it was clear, he turned onto the highway.

Almost immediately a car was on his bumper. Jarred looked down at the speedometer and saw he was going twenty-five. That was slow, he knew, but it felt fast to him. He eased the truck up to forty.

His heart was pounding as he gripped the wheel, feeling like a kid learning to drive. "I hope you appreciate this, Victoria," he growled, "because it's hell."

After a few miles, his confidence returned, though he kept staring at the shiny new cars. The houses and other buildings along the roadway seemed weird, too. Macky Bean's shack and the toilets at a campground were the only structures he'd laid eyes on in years.

Jarred could tell he was close to Edgar when the topography started getting familiar. He passed the service station where he used to stop for gas. Memories started flowing in his head. He felt as if he had risen from the dead.

But his excitement was dampened by his fear that something awful had happened to Victoria. She had come to mean so much to him, that he couldn't let it end now. He had to find her, to talk to her, to tell her he loved her.

He came to the turnoff to Edgar. Most of what he saw seemed familiar, yet in a way alien. He passed the bait shop where he used to get his fishing supplies. He wondered when he'd start recognizing people and if anyone would recognize him.

Mrs. Nesbit's big old house was on the right. It was decorated with Christmas lights. He'd forgotten about Christmas. Driving past, he realized Mrs. Nesbit had never strung up lights before. There was a big tree in the front window, and a kid on the porch. It occurred to him then that Mrs. Nesbit didn't live there anymore.

Jarred passed the street leading to his mother's house, and he peered up it, a lump forming in his throat. He half expected to see his mother's Chevy coming along, with her at the wheel.

Moments later he came to the downtown section. The buildings he'd known as a youth were all there and one or two new ones had sprung up. Jarred pulled over and gazed up the street, his eyes seeking out evidence of Victoria. It occurred to him then that he didn't know where to begin looking for her. Should he stop someone on the street and ask?

Jarred got out of the car. The street was completely deserted. He was still wearing his buckskin coat and he considered leaving it in the truck, so as not to draw attention to himself, but then he decided the attention would come no matter what. Once people realized who he was, he'd no doubt create a sensation.

He walked along the sidewalk, passing several vacant stores, until he came to the bar. It didn't look the way he remembered. There was a new sign on the front with a new name. He couldn't recall what the old one was, but he could hear laughter coming from inside, so he knew he'd find some people he could ask about Victoria.

Jarred pulled the door open. He could hardly see a thing except for the mirror with the Christmas lights behind the bar and the shadowy shapes of people. He stepped inside, noticing that the voices dwindled till there was nothing but silence.

He glanced around, able to see faces as his eyes adjusted. There were maybe six people—a big guy with a beard behind the bar who looked vaguely familiar, a middle-aged woman he didn't recognize sitting with an older man at the far end of the bar, two younger guys at a table, and then another man at the near end of the bar. The last face was terribly familiar. It was Steve Parnell's.

"Jesus H...." Parnell said, his mouth dropping open. He slammed the bottle of beer he'd been holding down on the bar and got to his feet.

Everybody was staring at Jarred. Nobody said a word.

Jarred looked at Parnell. "Where's Victoria?" he demanded.

"Boys," Parnell said, glancing around the bar, "you know who just dropped in to say howdy?"

"Where's Victoria?" Jarred roared.

"It's the wild man nobody but me said existed," Parnell crowed. "Take a good look at him, folks. This is Jarred Wilde. Beard's been shaved off, but it's him."

"Good God!"

"That really him?"

Jarred looked at their gawking faces. "Somebody please tell me what's happened to Victoria."

"What's the matter, Wilde," Parnell said, "get lonely without your girlfriend? Decide you liked the sweet stuff enough you had to come after it?"

Jarred took a deep breath to calm himself. "Just tell me where she is, Parnell."

"Wilde, I wouldn't give you the time of day."

They glared at each other as the bartender walked up to Jarred. "You really are Jarred Wilde," he said, shaking his head incredulously. "Don't know if you remember me. Dan Hanson's the name. We played some ball together."

Jarred knew he looked familiar. He took the proffered hand. "Oh, yeah, hello, Dan. Do you know anything about the girl they came for in the helicopter? Her name's Victoria."

"Yeah, everybody's heard. The sheriff's people picked her up."

"Where is she now?"

The bartender gave him the once-over as if Jarred were some kind of ghost. "They questioned her, but didn't hold her. She stayed with Anna Norton last night 'cause they didn't want her leavin' town. Maybe Steve's the one to ask about what's goin' on. She's bringin' charges against him." He glanced back at Steve Parnell, who sauntered over to where they stood.

There was hatred in Parnell's eyes, and it was easy to see he was well on his way to being drunk. "You know, Wilde," he slurred, "I don't believe I'm actually seein' you. I spent years combing the woods, trying to find your ass, and then you come waltzing right into town."

Jarred ignored the gibe, turning to Dan Hanson. "Where does Anna Norton live?"

Parnell poked Jarred in the chest. "Hey, caveman. I'm talkin' to you. There's a reason why I've been looking for you all these years and you know what it is, don't you?"

Jarred looked into Parnell's eyes, his antipathy rising. He remained silent.

"You killed my brother, you sonovabitch! And you ran off because of it."

"Come on, Steve," the bartender said, taking his arm. "Let's cool down."

Parnell jerked free. "The hell with that! I'm going to make this bastard pay!"

Dan Hanson tried to get hold of Parnell again. Parnell gave him a hard shove and the bartender tripped, falling over backward. Then, without warning, Parnell punched Jarred in the stomach, doubling him over.

The wind knocked out of him, Jarred looked up. Parnell was standing there red-faced, his fists clenched. He swung again, clipping Jarred on the side of the head and spinning him around.

Everybody in the room got to their feet. There were shouts of excitement. The bartender got up and just as he started for Parnell, people held him back. Parnell came at Jarred again, punching him repeatedly. Then he suddenly backed off, his face scarlet.

"What's the matter, Wilde?" he wheezed. "You afraid?"

"Fight him, Jarred!" somebody yelled when Parnell raised his fist again.

"No," Jarred said. "I don't want to hurt him."

Parnell laughed. "Who you gonna hurt, big fella? Me?"

He threw a big roundhouse right. Jarred ducked and grabbed Parnell from behind, pinning his arm behind him. "I told you to stop," he said into his ear. "Are you going to make me knock you down to understand?"

Parnell tried to twist free, but Jarred was too strong for him. When he gave up, Jarred shoved him toward

Dan Hanson. The bartender made Parnell sit down on a stool.

Jarred wiped a smudge of blood from the corner of his mouth. "Now," he said to the crowd generally. "How do I find Victoria?"

"Why don't I give them a call over at Anna's, Jarred? You can sit down and have a beer on the house."

"Okay, but call her now, Dan. Please."

The bartender put his arm around Parnell's shoulder. "What say you go on home, old buddy? There's too much bad blood for you both to be here."

Parnell reluctantly went with Hanson to the door, and staggered into the daylight. The bartender then took Jarred by the arm and led him to a table in back while the other customers stood staring.

"Guess it's been a while since you had a beer, partner," he said. "What'll you have?"

"Call Victoria for me," he replied. "She's the only reason I came back."

15

VICTORIA TOOK a walk along the river. She'd gone a mile or so from Anna's house, and had just turned back when she heard the siren. Through the trees she could see a sheriff's car over on the highway, its lights flashing, as it sped toward Edgar. The sight made her nervous. She'd had enough of the police to last for quite a while.

Actually, her experience hadn't been too bad, at least not after she'd given her statement. The deputy handling the case, the one in the Western hat who'd made the arrest, told her that Steve Parnell's story had been suspect all along. They had been working under the theory that he might even have been responsible for her disappearance. They asked her to stick around a few days until the district attorney had reviewed the case. She had all but been told not to worry.

Everyone she'd talked to was more interested in hearing about Jarred than they were about her or Parnell. "What's he really like?" they asked. She'd heard the question a hundred times.

Victoria refused to discuss Jarred except to say he was a solitary individual who asked only to be left alone. She hoped that people might leave him in peace, but wasn't optimistic. Half a dozen reporters had telephoned and one had come to Anna's door. Victoria refused to talk to them, except to plead for Jarred's privacy. Evidently her pleas fell on deaf ears.

Believing Jarred would need an advocate in Edgar, she had talked to Anna about him at some length and asked the woman to let her know if she heard any news of him.

"What do you plan to do, honey?" Anna had asked as they'd eaten the night before. "Are you going back to California?"

"I guess so. Once things are cleared up here, there's no point in staying—not if I can't see Jarred."

"Maybe he'll think better of living alone and come down out of the mountains."

Victoria had shaken her head. "No, I don't think so."

"He might be upset about your having been taken away."

"I'm sure he wasn't pleased. We both knew it would end one day. We'd come to an understanding." Victoria's eyes had brimmed with tears. Anna didn't ask any questions, instinctively understanding.

By the time she made it back to Anna Norton's house, the wind had kicked up and snow flurries were beginning to fall. As she went up the walkway of the old clapboard house, she saw Anna in the window. The woman threw open the door before Victoria made it to the top of the steps.

"Jarred's come back, honey!" she said breathlessly. "They called from the bar half an hour ago. He's there, and is asking for you!"

Victoria's heart rose into her throat. "Oh, my God!"

"I think you'd better get over there. Apparently there has already been some trouble with Steve Parnell. The sheriff was called."

So that was the siren she'd heard! Fear dampened her excitement. Victoria ran to her car, which was parked just down the street. She'd gotten her things back the day before, so she had on her own clothes and the coat that Jarred had made for her.

She drove to the downtown area. The main drag was a zoo. Fifteen or twenty vehicles were in the street, including both of Edgar's police cruisers. There were a hundred people or so, most of them gathered outside the bar.

Victoria parked and hurried to the bar. Passing one of the police cars, she saw Steve Parnell in the back seat, his head lowered. A couple of deputies were at the entrance to the bar. Victoria recognized one as a member of the detail that had arrested her.

"Hello, Miss Ross," he said, drawing himself up. "Glad you're here."

"What happened?"

"There was an altercation between Jarred Wilde and Steve Parnell earlier. Steve went home, got his rifle and came back gunning for Jarred. He fired, but missed. Nobody was hurt."

"Thank God. Where's Jarred now?"

"Inside. He's been waiting for you."

Victoria pushed her way in the door, searching the dark interior. A deputy was sitting at the bar, talking to the bartender. Jarred wasn't with them.

"Where is he?" she demanded.

The officer pointed toward the back of the bar. Peering into the gloom, she saw a man rise from his chair. He was the right size and shape, but his beard was gone, his hair had been hacked short.

"What happened to you?" she asked incredulously, searching the face she only half knew.

"Trying to keep up with fashion." He smiled and held out his arms to her.

Laughing, she threw herself at him. They kissed and he spun her around and around.

"I'm so happy to see you," he murmured. "Are you all right? You don't know how worried I've been."

Victoria put her hands on his clean-shaven cheeks. "I'm fine. Let me look at you," she said.

"What do you think?"

Jarred had been transformed. She was amazed to think this gorgeous hunk was the same man she'd come to love. "Looks like you need a little more practice with a razor." She gently touched a cut on his chin, then took her hands and pulled his head down until his mouth was over hers. "What made you come?" she whispered.

"You did, Victoria. I couldn't let you go." He kissed her again, so long and hard that she forgot that they weren't alone. When she finally pulled back, tears were in her eyes.

"I didn't think I'd ever see you again."

"I thought about your ranch," he said. "I wanted to see the place where you grew up. And I thought about what you said about forgiving myself. You were right. Teaching me that was the reason you came into my life."

She got up on her toes and kissed his cheek, marveling at its smoothness. It was all so incredible. A life with him had seemed hopeless, impossible, yet here he was. "As soon as they let us, we're going to get out of here, Jarred. I want to take you home."

"First, I need to talk to them about Steve. I don't want them to put him in jail."

"Why not?"

"You were right about me making peace with myself. I have to try to make peace with Steve, too. Even when we were fighting, I wouldn't let myself hit him. I knew that was very important."

Victoria smiled. "You're amazing. I love you so very much, Jarred."

"And I love you, too." He hugged her, twisting back and forth as he stroked her head. "Now that I'm here, I'm glad. But people really are strange. They ask a lot of questions and they all talk at the same time. Is it always like this?"

She laughed. "I think at first we'll be taking lots of walks in the woods."

He took her face in his hands and gazed at her with his wonderful blue eyes. "This ranch of yours doesn't have a cave on it by any chance, does it?"

"No. We can always turn out the lights, build a fire in the fireplace and pretend."

A Note from Janice Kaiser

The first books I fell in love with were the fairy tales I read as a child. I was captivated by stories of witches and goblins, handsome princes and sweet-tempered maidens who lived in lands where good and evil were clearly defined, and where happy endings were the order of the day.

And for me, the most romantic fairy tale of all was *Beauty and the Beast*. My heart was wrenched by the plight of the poor beast who lived isolated from the world—alone, unloved and misunderstood.

My hero in *Wilde at Heart* is like the beast in that fairy tale in so many ways. Jarred, too, is alone in the world—cut off from civilization, and hungering for companionship and love. When Victoria comes into his life, she must learn to look beyond his rough physical appearance to find the sensitive, caring man who is worthy of her love. And in my story, like the fairy tale, the happy ending has a moral: If you look beneath the surface of things, you might be surprised by what you find. You might even discover true love.

Books by Janice Kaiser

HARLEQUIN TEMPTATION
406—HEARTTHROB
417—THE MAVERICK

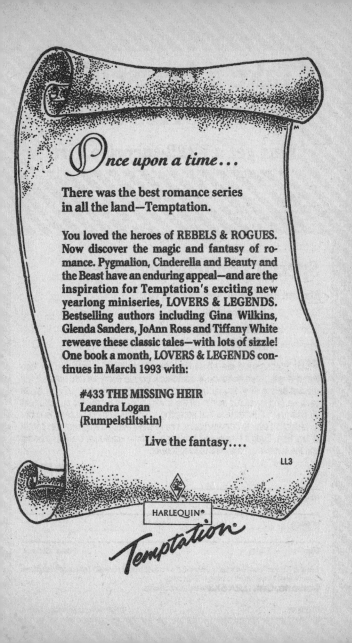

$\mathcal{O}$nce upon a time...

There was the best romance series in all the land—Temptation.

You loved the heroes of REBELS & ROGUES. Now discover the magic and fantasy of romance. Pygmalion, Cinderella and Beauty and the Beast have an enduring appeal—and are the inspiration for Temptation's exciting new yearlong miniseries, LOVERS & LEGENDS. Bestselling authors including Gina Wilkins, Glenda Sanders, JoAnn Ross and Tiffany White reweave these classic tales—with lots of sizzle! One book a month, LOVERS & LEGENDS continues in March 1993 with:

#433 THE MISSING HEIR
Leandra Logan
(Rumpelstiltskin)

Live the fantasy....

LL3

HARLEQUIN®

Temptation

Take 4 bestselling love stories FREE

Plus get a FREE surprise gift!

Special Limited-time Offer

Mail to Harlequin Reader Service®

P.O. Box 609
Fort Erie, Ontario
L2A 5X3

YES! Please send me 4 free Harlequin Temptation® novels and my free surprise gift. Then send me 4 brand-new novels every month, which I will receive before they appear in bookstores. Bill me at the low price of $2.69 each—a savings of 30¢ apiece off the cover prices, plus only 49¢ per shipment for delivery. * I understand that accepting the books and gift places me under no obligation ever to buy any books. I can always return a shipment and cancel at any time. Even if I never buy another book from Harlequin, the 4 free books and the surprise gift are mine to keep forever.

342 BPA AJHS

Name _____ (PLEASE PRINT)

Address _____ Apt. No. _____

City _____ Province _____ Postal Code _____

This offer is limited to one order per household and not valid to present Harlequin Temptation® subscribers.
*Terms and prices are subject to change without notice.
Canadian residents add applicable federal and provincial taxes.

CTEMP-93   ©1990 Harlequin Enterprises Limited

Harlequin is proud to present our best authors, their best books and the best for your reading pleasure!

Throughout 1993, Harlequin will bring you exciting books by some of the top names in contemporary romance!

In February, look for *Twist of Fate* by

Hannah Jessett had been content with her quiet life. Suddenly she was the center of a corporate battle with wealthy entrepreneur Gideon Cage. Now Hannah must choose between the fame and money an inheritance has brought or a love that may not be as it appears.

Don't miss TWIST OF FATE ...
wherever Harlequin books are sold.

BOB1

$\mathcal{O}$nce upon a time...

THERE WAS A FABULOUS
PROOF-OF-PURCHASE OFFER
AVAILABLE FROM

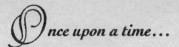

As you enjoy your Harlequin Temptation LOVERS & LEGENDS stories each and every month during 1993, you can collect four proofs of purchase to redeem a lovely opal pendant! The classic look of opals is always in style, and this necklace is a perfect complement to any outfit!

One proof of purchase can be found in the back pages of each LOVERS & LEGENDS title ... one every month during 1993!

LIVE THE FANTASY...

Lovers & Legends

NAME: _____

ADDRESS: _____

_____

CITY: _____

STATE/PROVINCE: _____

ZIP/POSTAL CODE: _____

ONE PROOF OF PURCHASE   084 KAO LLPOPR